DATING
DO-OVER

RealTV
TAKE FOUR

DATING
DO-OVER

WENDY LAWTON

MOODY PUBLISHERS
CHICAGO

Library of Congress Cataloging-in-Publication Data

Lawton, Wendy.
    Dating do-over / Wendy Lawton.
        p. cm. — (Real TV—real transformations series ; take 4)
    Summary: With a little help from the television show "Dating
Do-Over," seventeen-year-old Bailey tries to learn to interact with boys
and find a prom date, while also relying on her Christian faith to help
her become a better person.
    ISBN-13: 978-0-8024-5416-4
    [1. Interpersonal relations—Fiction. 2. Self-confidence—Fiction.
3. Reality television programs—Fiction. 4. Proms—Fiction.
5. Christian life—Fiction.] I. Title.

PZ7.L4425Dat 2005
[Fic]—dc22

                                                      2005004077

                        ISBN: 0-8024-5416-X
                     ISBN-13: 0-8024-5416-4

                   1 3 5 7 9 10 8 6 4 2

              Printed in the United States of America

For all the high school Sunday school students
I've had at Hilmar Covenant over the years.
How I've learned from you.

Contents

Real TV

Real TV

Acknowledgments

Special thanks to The Learning Channel, Style Network, and BBC television programs that spawned the concept for the *Real TV* series. For *Dating Do-Over*, I was inspired by *The Date Patrol* and *Makeover Story*. The creators of these programs—despite the fun and fluff—take the concept of makeover much deeper.

And, as always, big thanks to Andrew McGuire and the incomparable editorial and design team at Moody Publishers and to my agent and friend, Janet Grant.

RealTV

Dateless & Defeated

1

Thursday, March 31st

To: AskAngela@MetroGirlZine
From: Dateless&Defeated@Wazoo.com

Dear Ask Angela,
   I need help. It's exactly six weeks and two days until prom. I'm still dateless and getting more desperate with each day. According to *Metro Girl Zine* u have all the answers. What advice can u give a klutzy, clumsy, socially backward senior who hates to miss her last

chance to ever attend a high school prom? I'm attaching a photo so u can see that I don't have any obvious warts or missing front teeth. The red hair is natural. I'm five foot even and weigh 105 pounds—nothing out of the ordinary. I can't figure out what it is that makes me the perennial wallflower. Can u offer any pointers that'll help me catch a certain someone's eye?

Thanks in advance,
Dateless and Defeated

✳   ✳   ✳

Bailey hit the "send" button and closed the lid on her laptop. *There. We'll see if I ever hear back from Ask Angela.* She wondered if Angela really existed at all. Wouldn't it be weird if some old guy with hair growing out of his ears answered the e-mails? Who'd know? Oh well, it didn't matter. And just to be safe, she had used an e-mail alias as a return address. She felt better for having written, like she'd taken action instead of sitting around wringing her hands.

She opened her diary. There was the list of possible prom dates she started a few days ago. She had numbered one, two, and three, but couldn't bring herself to write in any names. Three numbered lines—blank. *So much for an action list.* She chewed on the end of her pencil. She knew precisely which name would go at the top of the list, but there was no sense kidding herself. Trevor would never ever ask her to the prom. Best leave the possibilities open for now. After all, it was *her* diary, and she could do what she wanted. If she actually penned the list, it would all be too depressing.

"Hey, Bay." Jenn opened the door without knocking. "Your mom said to come on up."

"Hi, Jenn." Bailey put her pencil down. "You're a welcome distraction." Jenn had been her best friend for years. She was the kind of friend who knew everything about you and still liked you.

"Writing in your journal again?"

Bailey nodded. "You know me, I always have to work things out in my journal. I barely even know what I'm thinking until I've started lining it out on paper."

Jenn leaned over Bailey's shoulder to look at the page. "Uh oh. You're obsessing about prom again."

"I wouldn't exactly call it obsessing."

Jenn snorted. No one could ever call her subtle.

"Okay. Maybe just a little." Bailey turned sideways in her chair and draped her arm over the back. "Mom keeps telling me to ask one of the guys from church." She gave an exaggerated shudder. "Yeah, right. Like it wouldn't be hard enough to go on a formal date, let alone take a stranger who knows not one solitary soul aside from me."

"Not quite. I'd know your date if you asked someone from church. So would Luke and Jace." She and Bailey both went to the same church—San Vincente Christian. "But you're right. If you go with someone from school they'll have their own group of friends at the prom in case things get awkward." Jenn flopped on the bed, stomach down. As always, her feet were near the headboard and her head toward the end of the bed, close to Bailey's desk. This had been her favorite position ever since she started coming over in fourth grade. She took one of Bailey's wisteria corduroy pillows and bent it in half to prop herself up.

"Why do they have to put this kind of pressure on us anyway?" Bailey asked, not expecting an answer. She really didn't even know who "they" were. "Like it's not hard enough to try to measure up." Bailey closed her diary. "No, they need to make getting a date another rite of passage."

"Rite of passage?" Jenn made a face. "You've been reading too many of Ms. Barnard's coming-of-age novels."

"What do you mean 'too many'? They happen to be assigned. How can you not read them?"

"Oh, stop," Jenn said. "Let's not get off track talking about English Lit instead of important stuff like dating and prom. Rite of passage or not, I know what you mean." Jenn rolled over onto her back and propped her feet up on the headboard. Her dark brown hair fanned out around her head. "A girl's social success or failure can be measured by this one test. It's like we're all being watched and sorted. If you don't get asked, you go into one pile. If you do get asked, but it's not a guy on the A-list, you go into another pile. If you end up asking someone outside of school, you go onto yet another heap. We won't even talk about those poor unfortunates who end up taking a brother or a cousin."

"Well, I'll tell you this," said Bailey crossing her arms, "if I get volunteered one more time for the prom decorating committee and end up on all fours, crawling around in filthy jeans when the first blissful couples began to arrive . . . ." She inhaled long and deeply. "Well, it doesn't even bear thinking."

How many times since she'd started at San Vincente High had Dad arrived to pick her up from a long day of turning a giant room into a winter wonderland, a vernal meadow, or a starry night? She'd always hurry into the car and slink down into the front seat next to Dad, wishing she were invisible. As they pulled out of the parking lot, they'd invariably pass car after car filled with happy couples dressed for the "evening to remember." How often she wished hers was an "evening to forget," but somehow she could always play back the details of those promless nights like a slow-mo movie.

"You can come with Jace and me—we're cool. You know Jace and I are mostly friends. We'd have fun."

"Thanks, but that would be way too weird." Sometimes a group of girls decided to go together without dates, but going as a threesome was not what she planned for her senior year. Besides, Jace might be more friend than boyfriend to Jenn at this point, but Bailey knew her friend was open to growing the relationship.

"Well, don't despair *yet*," Jenn said hopefully.

Apparently Jenn figured there would be plenty of time to despair later. Bailey hated this helpless feeling. Who ever decided that boys needed to ask girls anyway? Face it, most of the boys in her school were far less capable than the girls when it came to making plans, asking someone, and working out the details.

"I mean lots of guys wait until the last minute," Jenn said.

"Yeah. Well, I'm not going to panic." Who was she kidding? She was already in mid-panic. Her friends talked of little else than prom these days. Besides, she knew that the later you waited to look for a dress, the more picked-over the racks. Her school was one of the last ones in the area to hold their prom. By the time she looked for a dress she'd be lucky to find one without the telltale sweat stains that meant it had been worn and returned. *Yuck.*

"Good attitude, not panicking," Jenn said in her most encouraging voice. "Besides, guys can spot desperation a mile away. They can smell it."

"Thank you for sharing that." Bailey wished she could just change the subject, but these days, prom was *the* subject. "I don't know why I'm even stressing. It's probably all for the best anyway. I'm such a klutz. What makes me think I could go on a real date without tripping over my own hem, spilling my drink down the front of my dress, and saying nothing but stupid things?"

Jenn threw the wisteria pillow at Bailey's head. "You stop. That kind of talk is dangerous. Words have power, y'know. If you don't watch out, you'll have yourself believing that." Jenn worked as a peer counselor at school. Self-deprecating talk had become one of her pet peeves. She believed a connection existed between self put-downs and poor performance.

"I know you're right about the negative talk, but you've seen how tongue-tied I get around guys. It's like I start to stammer and all kinds of dumb things get blurted out." Bailey chewed on a fingernail.

"You just need practice."

"No duh." Bailey got up from her desk and plopped down on the bed next to her friend. "So tell me, wise one, when one cannot seem to get a date, how does one practice dating?"

"I mean you need to practice talking to boys. It's about getting comfortable—about familiarity. It's tough since you don't even have a brother. It's no wonder you have trouble."

Jenn was right. Except for Dad, theirs was a female household. The ladies had consisted of Mom and her for the longest time. Mallory was three years old and Madeline was two. Bailey called them her M&Ms. Not a trace of boy genes in the whole family.

Jenn sat up, nearly knocking Bailey off the bed. "I know what we'll do."

"Do? About what?"

"About solving your problem," Jenn said. "I mean you need to become date-worthy before we can expect some guy to bite. We totally need to fix you."

"Bite, huh? I think you're mixing your metaphors. Is this a fishing expedition or am I to be on someone's menu?"

"Don't try to distract me with terminology." Jenn pressed her lips together.

Bailey recognized the look—her friend was on a mission. When she got that look, there would be no stopping her. "Okay, how do you propose to fix me?"

"Maybe fix is the wrong word. It's too mild." Jenn spread her arms wide. "We are going to reinvent you, girlfriend."

Bailey groaned. The last time Jenn initiated a Bailey-project, they'd both ended up grounded for two weeks. To be fair, it was in fifth grade, and the horses hadn't been injured and . . .

Jenn lowered her head and looked at Bailey through squinted eyes. "If you are going to bring up that circus incident, I don't want to hear it." The two girls had known each other for so long that it seemed as if Jenn could read Bailey's mind. "Besides, this plan does not involve live animals."

Bailey laughed. "So you're promising that no animals will be harmed in the reinvention of Bailey Tollefson?"

Jenn laughed.

Bailey didn't mind the idea of reinventing herself. *If it works, I'm there.* She envied the ease Jenn enjoyed in her friendships with guys. And it wasn't just that Jenn was pretty. Growing up with a twin brother meant Jenn spent most of her waking hours with the opposite sex. "You are lucky having Luke. You started hanging with a boy before you were even born."

"You're right. Having a boy for a womb mate totally dismantled the male mystique for me." It gave Jenn plenty of practice talking to the opposite sex. Of course anyone could talk to Luke. He was the best listener. Everyone loved him.

"I need to go home." Jenn stood up.

"But you just got here. I thought you were going to help reinvent me."

"I know, but I'm serious about this project. I want to go home and map out our plan. We're going to take this one step at a time."

Bailey groaned. "So when will I find out the details?"

"Let's meet in the cafeteria before school. I'll buy you a bagel, and we'll get started right away." Jenn headed out the door and down the stairs before Bailey could ask any more questions.

"Bye," Bailey said to the empty room.

Mom stuck her head into the room. "Were you talking to me?"

"No. I was just waving good-bye to Jenn's vapor trail," Bailey said.

"That was a quick visit."

"Jenn's on a mission to make me popular in time for the prom."

"Have you decided to go?" Mom asked.

Bailey hardly knew how to answer. As if deciding

could get her a date. "I haven't exactly been invited, Mom."

"Well, surely if your friends knew you wanted to go, someone would invite you, right?" Mom picked up a gum wrapper that had missed the waste can. "Or you can ask one of the kids from church."

"That doesn't work for a lot of reasons." Bailey didn't want to go into detail with her mom. "I'd really like to go with someone from school."

"I hope you decide soon so we have time to shop."

Sometimes it seemed as if her mom didn't get it. No, that wasn't fair. Nobody loved her as much as her parents, but sometimes . . .

"Okay, Mom. As soon as I know something I'll let you know." Even as she said it, she knew her mom would make the dress and shoes happen no matter how late.

"I need to run out and pick up milk. I can't believe I forgot to check the fridge before your dad left his office." Mom stepped out into the hall. "Will you watch your sisters and keep an eye on the sauce? I turned the burner down so it should be fine without your having to do anything."

"Sure." Her sisters would provide a much-needed distraction. She followed her mom downstairs.

She heard the high voices of "let's pretend" coming from the family room. As she came into the room she saw that both girls had their toys and crayons spread out around the coffee table. "How are my sweet M&Ms?" She picked up Madeline's hand and planted a smoochie kiss on her palm.

Mallory giggled at the word M&Ms. It was one of her favorite candies and her favorite pet name. The same tired joke never got old when you were three years old.

Madeline wore a net tutu pulled crookedly over her jeans. "Dance, Bay-we." She put her hands up and stepped onto Bailey's feet.

"Mallory, can you put on the music for us?" Bailey waltzed with short steps so she wouldn't knock her sister off. After they'd danced halfway across the family room, Mallory finally got the cassette player going. The music started midway through "The Three Little Kittens."

"My turn now," Mallory said, following them as they danced. "Pick me. Pick me," she repeated in a singsong voice.

"Your turn will come," Bailey said, watching her impatient little sister hop from foot to foot. Bailey had to smile. *Is that how I look to guys? Pick me. Pick me.* Somehow she knew exactly how Mallory felt. "Come here." She stopped dancing. "Madeline, squeeze both feet here." She pointed to her left foot. "Hold on to my waist. We'll put Mallory over here so we can all dance together." Mallory put both her feet on Bailey's right foot. As the first bars of "Farmer in the Dell" played, the threesome lurched into the dance.

They danced until the tops of Bailey's feet tingled with the weight of her sisters. Why couldn't she stop wondering about the plan Jenn was hatching? As she tumbled onto the couch with her two laughing partners, she wondered if a prom threesome might not be a lot safer in the long run than whatever her friend had in mind.

RealTV

Pathetic Pollster

2

To: AskAngela@MetroGirlZine
From: PatheticPollster@Wazoo.com

Dear Ask Angela,

   U probably have not had time to read my e-mail from yesterday, but I figured I better give u an update. I'm the one who needed pointers on how to catch the attention of potential prom dates. Maybe that shouldn't be plural— there's one guy in particular. Anyway, before u could send an answer, my friend stepped in with a plan. She thinks much of my problem is that I'm uncomfortable around boys and they sense it. U will never believe what she cooked up to help me . . .

❋   ❋   ❋

Bailey rested her hands on the keyboard. How could she explain what Jenn had called "Step One"? As she thought about the plan, she smiled. *Leave it to Jenn. The idea had potential, but . . .*

She put her hands back on the keyboard and began to type. After about ten minutes, she typed in the signature of her new alias: Pathetic Pollster. Before she could waste the next hour reading and rereading her e-mail, she closed her eyes and pressed the "send" button. Who knew if Ask Angela would ever reply, but it felt good getting the whole thing written out. It helped her sort out the good from the ghastly. The day had started innocently enough . . .

❋   ❋   ❋

As she spotted Jenn in the cafeteria, Bailey knew her friend had big plans before a word had even been spoken. There, sitting beside the toasted bagels, were two containers of cream cheese. Jenn never *ever* remembered to ask for it. The presence of that cream cheese spoke volumes. Jenn had planned this reinvention right down to the bribe she knew she'd need in order to get Bailey to go along with her plan. If Bailey had any sense, she'd have walked out of there.

22

"Bailey," Jenn said as she stood up, "have a bagel while we talk."

It was a bribe all right, but who could resist strawberry-flavored cream cheese? Bailey sat down and opened the container. Okay, the bribe worked. That's what came of long friendships. Your friend ended up knowing enough about you to make her downright dangerous.

"Hey, Jenn." Luke came up to the table. "You went by the bagel store? Did you get me a bagel?"

"No. This is an important meeting."

"Sorry," he said, taking a bite of Jenn's bagel. "Hi, Bailey."

"Hi, Luke." Bailey knew she should have said something else—something witty and funny—but she couldn't think of a single thing to say. If she couldn't talk comfortably with Luke, how could she hope to talk to any other boy?

"Are you planning any special April Fool's jokes today?" Luke asked.

"April Fool's?" Jenn stopped chewing. "I'd forgotten it was April first. We do not have time for messing around."

"Sounds like you two are on a mission." Luke turned and waved at Jace coming in the door.

"Yum. Bagels and cream cheese." Jace slid into the seat next to Jenn. "Do you want that second half?"

"You guys." Jenn's voice rose. "We're trying to have a meeting here."

"Prom decorating committee?" Luke crooked his finger to scrape the remains of the cream cheese from the tiny plastic cup.

Bailey gave Jenn a look that said, "See?" Just like she suspected, she would forever be branded as the prom decorator. It was like the old lament *always a bridesmaid, never a bride*—only her lament was *always a prom-maid, never the prom*.

"No," Jace said, "the first prom decorating meeting isn't until April 15th, that's two weeks from today."

"Yikes! That only gives the committee a month," Bailey said. Even though she wanted to be part of more than just decorating for prom, she knew she'd still be on the committee.

"Anyway guys," Jenn said, "we need to get to work if we are going to get anything accomplished before class. Will you leave if we each give you a half of our bagel?"

"Sure," Luke said with a smile. "Especially since it includes strawberry cream cheese."

Bailey handed Luke the top half of her bagel. Jace took the bottom of Jenn's.

"Thanks," Jace said. "See you in class."

When the guys left, Jenn turned toward Bailey. "Pretend those were real guys. What went wrong with that encounter?"

"What do you mean *real guys*? What's not real about them?"

"I mean dateable guys."

Bailey didn't mention that Jenn *was* dating Jace and that there was no shortage of girls who'd give anything to date Luke. Both guys were completely dateable, but Jenn meant guys on Bailey's nonexistent prom list.

"So what went wrong?" Bailey asked.

"You hardly said a word." Jenn raised her voice since the cafeteria got noisier and noisier the closer it got to first period. "You've got to learn to talk to guys, Bailey."

"I don't know what to say. I mean I did say something about decorations."

"Yeah, half a dozen words. That doesn't help a conversation get started." Jenn took the last bite of her bagel. "That's where my plan comes in. You are going to learn how to approach guys and how to get them talking to you."

Bailey nearly choked on her bite of bagel. "I can't do that. I don't know what to say." She could hear her voice getting higher and higher. "What if I say something, and then they say something back, and I get tongue-tied?"

"Don't panic, I've got that covered." Jenn opened her backpack. She took out a clipboard and a stack of papers. "You know that assignment we have for Econ, to collect and analyze some kind of statistics?"

"Yeah?" Bailey didn't follow. Weren't they talking about Bailey's inability to communicate with the opposite sex? Not that she cared that Jenn changed the subject. She'd much rather talk about school than about boys.

"I designed a poll—that's my part of the assignment."

"Okay . . . ?" Bailey's voice rose slightly at the end of the word. "You did it by yourself?" When she and Jenn teamed together on an assignment, they'd always worked together every step of the way. Both girls hated group assignments when you couldn't choose your group because, too often, you'd end up with group members who were only along for the ride. The slackers would miss every meeting but still share equally in the grade. It had become a sore point with both girls.

"I'm not cutting you out here. You'll see why I went ahead with it. We're going to make this project do double duty. Besides, you are going to be the pollster."

Bailey started getting a funny feeling. Maybe Jenn hadn't changed the subject. "I'll bet I'm not going to like this, am I?"

"Don't start out with a negative attitude."

A group of kids came into the cafeteria laughing and talking loudly. Bailey looked over her shoulder. It was Trevor and a bunch of friends. He led them over to a nearby table. What was it about Trevor? Bailey wondered if he planned to attend prom. He always talked to her in English class, but she couldn't ask him about it without appearing to be fishing for a date. His ease and friendliness had always appealed to her. She knew she could have fun if she went with Trevor, but he'd probably never think of her that way. She focused back on Jenn. *What had they been talking about? Oh, yes, the poll.*

"Listen, we only have about ten minutes until class, so let me explain this to you. Just think of it as a school project, nothing more."

"And it is more?"

"Of course. As part of your reinvention I want you to get more comfortable talking to boys. This is how you're going to start." Jenn put a piece of paper into the clipboard and slid it over to Bailey. "You are going to poll as many of the boys as you can about what they look for in a date."

Bailey blinked hard.

"Hear me out. From an academic point of view, it will be an interesting study. When we present our findings, the class will love it—not like a poll on cafeteria food or how many books you read in a month or something. Right?"

"I guess so." Bailey knew the teacher would love it because it was out of the ordinary. Most kids came up with the same old polls. "I just want to know how I'm going to ask these questions when I can barely stammer out a word to most guys."

"It'll be easy because as far as they know, it's only a school assignment. Just ask the questions, mark down their answers, and thank them for their participation."

Bailey looked at the first question on the sheet. "So I just go up to a guy and say, 'Have you ever been out on a date?'" Bailey raised her eyebrows. "I don't think so."

Jenn sighed. "Not like that. You go up to someone and you say, 'Can I ask you a few questions for the poll we need to do for Econ?' Then it makes it nothing more than an assignment."

"An assignment, huh?"

"You always ace assignments. You'll go into your serious-student mode, and before you know it, you'll be talking to dozens of guys."

"I'm outta here." Bailey stood up to gather her things.

"Stop." Jenn stood up and looked Bailey straight in the eye. "Didn't I hear you say you wanted a date for the prom this year?"

"I did, but if it takes me approaching guys, I'm finished before I start."

"Just give it a try. Start out with easy guys and work up to the more threatening ones." Jenn waved her arm at Jace and Luke across the room. "Luke, Jace." She signaled for them to come over. "Just start with Luke and Jace. I'll do Jace so you can watch."

"Got more bagels?" Jace asked hopefully as he slid into the seat next to Jenn.

"No, but will you guys answer the questions for our Econ poll?" Jenn asked.

"Wow. You've already started on that assignment? You're way ahead," Jace said. "I'll go first."

"Have you ever been out on a date?" Jenn asked, looking professional.

Jace laughed. "I think so. Didn't we go to the prom last year?"

"I'll take that as a yes, then. So, what kind of date do you prefer: informal with a group of kids—a movie or event date; or a formal date—like a prom?" Jenn had her pencil ready.

"I don't know. I like to go out in a group, but we had fun at the prom."

"Which would you prefer?"

"I guess informal."

Jenn wrote that down. "So what kind of girl do you prefer to date—someone you've known a long time or someone new and exciting?"

"Oh man, I better get this right." Jace laughed. "How about someone I've known a long time who still seems new and exciting?"

Luke laughed. "Dude, you should be a politician."

"I guess I should put a blank for 'other,'" Jenn said. "I can see that there could be all kinds of answers. This creating a poll is harder than it looks." She finished asking all the questions of Jace and then put a fresh sheet of paper on the clipboard and handed it to Bailey. "Okay, Bailey, you ask Luke."

Bailey took the pencil and clipboard. "Have you ever been out on a date?"

"Yes," Luke said.

Bailey marked it on the sheet. This was Luke, Jenn's brother, and yet her hand still shook. *Stop it. This is just a school assignment. And Luke is like a brother.* She looked at Luke. He smiled in that encouraging way. That's what she liked about him. He was just plain nice. He acted the same toward the grandmas at church as he did toward the cutest girl in their class.

"Bailey," Jenn said, "ask the next question."

"Oh. Right." She looked at the clipboard. "So what kind of date do you prefer: informal with a group of kids—a movie or event date; or a formal date—like a prom?"

"Not formal. That's too much pressure. I like going out with a group, like when our whole group at church goes to a baseball game or something . . . but I do like one-on-one as well. I don't know."

Bailey didn't know what to write down. "Well, if you had to plan a date this very minute, what would you do?"

Jenn smiled. "Good restatement, Bailey. Remember we talked about that in Econ. That sometimes you had to restate the question but you'd need to restate it the same way each time in order for the data to be right?"

"I forgot about that." Bailey smiled. Maybe she could do this. It felt more and more like a real assignment.

Luke tapped his foot in a comical way. "Um, does anyone want me to answer the question?"

"Oops." Bailey laughed. "I forgot about you."

Luke laughed out loud and several heads turned their way. Bailey couldn't believe it. She said something that made a boy laugh.

"Back to your question," Luke said, pretending to be offended. "I guess if I had to plan a date this very minute, I'd pick the old standby, a movie, because it's easy to do on the spur of the moment. It takes a lot of work to get a group together."

"I hadn't thought about that," Bailey said. "Girls just usually wait and hope to be asked. I never thought about the whole organizational thing."

"Yeah, from a guy's point of view it can be a scary thing. You worry about whether they'll say yes. You worry about picking the right movie or the right activity. You worry about having enough money or having to share costs—"

"Hey," Jenn interrupted. "This is fun, but the bell's almost ready to ring, and we've only gotten through two questions on Luke's questionnaire."

"Why don't I catch you at lunch, Bailey, and I'll finish answering your questions."

"Okay. Thanks." Bailey couldn't believe it. It had felt so natural talking to Luke. Maybe Jenn was right. She just needed to think about it differently.

As she gathered up her things for class, she felt as if she'd made a tiny breakthrough. During break that morning she caught two other guys from class and polled them. They seemed to enjoy taking the poll. When you had an official function, it wasn't so hard to approach guys.

Before lunch, she went into the restroom to wash her hands and put on a little lip gloss. She hoped to get three or four guys polled before lunch was over. She looked at her reflection in the mirror. Good thing she'd worn her best jeans and her new sweater. Even her brooch seemed perfect. This was fun.

"There you are," Luke said as she got into the lunch line. He slipped in behind her. "Can I sit with you? You can ask the questions as we eat."

"Sure." Bailey felt some of that old shyness come back. Nearly four years in high school and she'd never once had a guy arrange to sit with her at lunch. *Stop. This is Luke. This is an assignment.* Why did she always have to make things bigger than they were? Boy, did she ever need Jenn's reinvention.

They got their trays and sat down.

"So," Bailey said, after she swallowed her first bite of taco. "What kind of girl do you prefer to date—someone you've known a long time or someone new and exciting?"

Luke was silent for a while. "That's a hard question the way you've phrased it. I don't know that I think about *kinds* when I think about girls. I mean I don't choose a category of girl. I get interested in a person."

Bailey tried to think of a way to restate it. "When you think of a person, do you tend to lean toward someone who's already a friend or are you intrigued by someone you don't know yet? Someone who's a little mysterious?"

"It would have to be someone I know because I decided long ago dating would not be a recreational activity for me. I mean the whole purpose of dating is getting to know someone who you may someday marry."

Bailey didn't say anything immediately, but Luke's answer surprised her. Talk about making something bigger than it was. "Doesn't that put an awful lot of pressure on you?"

"I guess so, but can you imagine how much trouble it would be if you started dating—just for fun—and you fell in love with a person who was not a Christian? That's why John and Susan didn't date at all. They believe courtship is a better way to find the person God wants you to have for your mate."

John was their youth pastor and Bailey had heard

him talk about courtship as an alternative to dating, but she'd never really considered it. She had such trouble communicating with guys that she spent most of her time just worrying about how to be friendly. For her, waiting for courtship seemed like the easy way out. "This morning you answered yes to the question about whether you date or not. Does that mean you don't plan to use courtship methods?"

"Courtship seems a little too complicated in a world that is so casual. I guess I plan to date carefully. Does that make any sense?"

"It's kind of like Jenn is doing, right? Where she and Jace are friends but she keeps things from getting too weird too fast."

"Nice way to put it." Luke laughed. "It's funny how freely I'm talking about this with you. I usually keep my opinions to myself since they seem so old-fashioned. Please don't put any of this into the survey. Just put that I like to date—how was it you put it—familiar friends?"

"Okay." Bailey checked that box. "But I like what you said. I guess the thought of dating is so scary for me that I never took time to think about the ideas behind dating."

"Why is dating scary to you?"

"I'm so terrible at communicating; I just freeze up. I get nervous and then I do something dorky. That's why Jenn is trying to reinvent me." Bailey laughed. "This poll may be an assignment, but Jenn is using it to push me to talk to guys."

"So you have trouble communicating with guys?" Luke looked at his watch. "Let's see, we've been talking for nearly fifteen minutes, and I didn't see you do a single dorky thing."

Bailey laughed. Luke was right. "Maybe you're just easy to talk to. Let me ask the rest of the questions before Jenn finds out how few questionnaires I've completed." She asked the rest of the questions, resisting the urge to stop and talk to Luke about his answers. She liked the way he thought.

"Is that all?" Luke asked when they'd finished.

"Yep. I'm done." As she pulled her papers together, she saw Trevor stand up a few tables away and take his tray.

"I know Jenn's intentions are good but don't let my sister do too much reinventing. Tell her I like you just the way you are."

Bailey didn't know what to say to that.

"Hey, Trev." Luke turned around and caught Trevor's sleeve as he walked past toward the tray drop-off. "Got a minute? Bailey needs you."

Bailey's mouth went dry. What was Luke thinking? Of all the guys in the room, Trevor was the hardest one of all.

"Sure," Trevor said. "Let me take my tray, and I'll be right back."

"I'll take your tray. I need to go," Luke said getting up and stacking Trevor's tray on top of his. "See you, Bay. It was fun talking to you."

Bailey gave a jerky kind of wave in Luke's direction. *Why did Luke's eye have to land on Trevor?*

Trevor sat down next to Bailey. "So, what do you need?"

Bailey's heart thumped. Could she get anything to come out of her mouth? "I'm taking a class." *Stupid.* At least her mouth worked, even if it didn't work well. "I mean we're doing a survey for that assignment in Econ class." There. That was better. She lowered her glasses, trying to look businesslike. "Would you mind asking a few questions?"

Trevor seemed uncomfortable. "Sure, if you tell me what questions to ask."

Bailey wished she could somehow disappear. "I meant answer a few questions." *Pull yourself together.* She remembered her success with Luke. She thought about her good jeans and the lip gloss. She remembered how easy it was with Luke. *I can do this. I'm prepared. It's an assignment.* "We're doing a poll on teen guys' dating preferences."

Trevor narrowed his eyes. "Is this an April Fool's joke?"

"No. It's really a poll." A few of Trevor's friends gathered. *Great.* She'd have to do this with an audience. "Here's the first question: Have you ever been out on a date?"

Trevor looked at his friends gathering around. "Are you sure this is not some kind of joke?"

One of the guys whistled. "Oooo, Trevie, she's going to ask you for a date."

"Go away," Trevor said to the guy. "Bailey, are you sure this is really a poll? I've already been fooled twice today, and I know these guys have something else up their sleeves."

She pushed the clipboard toward him. "It's really a poll, see . . . but let's not do it now. I'll ask you later . . . maybe in class."

"No, it's okay. I'm just jumpy." He turned toward her. "Yes, I date."

"What kind of date do you prefer?" She stopped to give him the choices.

"Hey, she's not only fishing for a date, she's trying to

34

get it planned at the same time," said one of the girls. Bailey didn't even turn around to see who said it.

"I'm going to get going, Trevor," she said, gathering her things. There was no way she could do this with a whole group of hecklers standing around. "I'll catch you later." As she stood, the edge of the clipboard caught her tray and upended it onto the bench between them. Clumps of salsa plopped on Trevor's pants and spattered his shirt. Trevor jumped up, smearing at his clothes with a wadded up napkin.

"Good going, Bailey," said one of the guys, trying to high-five her. "You managed to do what we were trying to do all day. April Fool's, Trevor!"

Bailey could feel prickles of heat creep up her neck. Had the cafeteria suddenly gone silent? "I—I'm sorry. I didn't mean . . . Here let me wipe—" As she threw her leg over the bench to stand up she noticed her own clothes. She had gotten spattered worse than Trevor.

"No!" Trevor backed up.

"You two look like accident survivors." The teacher who had lunchroom duty came over to offer a stack of paper towels.

Trevor looked at Bailey. "No, I don't think this was an accident, but I guess all is fair on April Fool's Day." He turned and walked toward the restroom leaving Bailey standing beside the table with her mouth gaping. Trevor's friends followed him.

"What happened?" Jenn came up behind her. "I saw this whole crowd, and there you were in the center."

"Do you think it's too late to apply for early graduation? I never want to come back here."

"You look like you're covered in blood. What is that?"

35

"Don't ask."

"I don't get it. Everyone's saying you got Trevor with the perfect April Fool's Day joke by catching him with his guard down. What did you do?"

Bailey didn't answer. She gathered her things, stuffed the clipboard in her backpack, and left the cafeteria. So much for improving her communication with guys.

RealTV

Blind but Beautiful

3

To: AskAngela@MetroGirlZine
From: BlindButBeautiful@Wazoo.com

Dear Ask Angela,

OK, I know u haven't had time to answer either of my two letters, but writing u helps me sort things out in my mind. I'm the one who was obsessing about a prom date. Remember? My friend is trying to remake me. Happily, a whole weekend has gone by since I spilled a tray of cafeteria food on the guy I once hoped would ask me. Some way to catch a guy's attention, huh?

Well, today my friend decided we were going to go for shock value and get rid of my brainy looks (her words) and try for a dreamy, feminine look (again, her words). She came to my house early and worked on my hair, makeup, and clothes. Jenn is good at that stuff. The trouble came when she insisted I go without glasses . . .

❀   ❀   ❀

How could she explain in an e-mail how klutzy she was?

Yesterday she went to Jenn's house to watch one of their favorite shows, *Dating Do-Over*. Each week the show featured a dating failure and turned them into a success. Bailey and Jenn liked the show, but they felt more connected because it was filmed right in Burbank and because Luke worked on the set. His title was "Grip." He laughed when they asked him for insider information. He said though the title sounded important, he was just a helper on the set. He moved things around, cleaned up, and ran errands. But according to him, it was the perfect after-school job.

Last night's episode featured a woman who laughed too loud and hogged all the conversation. After a few minutes of watching her, it was obvious what the problem was.

"She is too overwhelming," Jenn said. "Can you see the guys backing away from her?"

"Yeah, she'd scare anyone. Her makeup is too strong, her clothes are too wild . . . even her body movements are exaggerated." But Bailey wished she had a little of this woman's confidence.

"Even Kiely Kimmel backs off slightly as the woman talks," Jenn said. "Watch." Kiely Kimmel was the host of *Dating Do-Over*. She was a master at getting guests to see their mistakes without making them feel attacked. "I'd love to have her job. It must be such fun to organize the makeovers and help people discover their mistakes."

Bailey didn't say anything. Jenn's big plan for the reinvention of Bailey was a Kiely Kimmel kind of project for sure. As Bailey watched, she could see the gradual transformation. They used Victor Rocco, an acting coach, to teach the woman to soften her voice, soften her movements, and tone down her presence. It made a huge difference. But when Claudia Michael, the stylist, redid her clothes, her hair, and her makeup, the transformation was complete.

"That's what we need to do," Jenn said, as the credits rolled and the theme song faded.

"What? Go on *Dating Do-Over*?"

"No," said Jenn. "Though it wouldn't be a bad idea to try . . ."

"What did you mean then? What do we need to do?"

"We need to do a makeover on you. Look at the difference that the woman's makeover made. Look at the attention she received from the change."

"How does a makeover help me get a date for the prom?"

"I'm thinking you look so intelligent, you may be scaring guys off."

"That's a stereotypical thing to say. Do you really think guys are so shallow that they'd be scared off by the appearance of brains?" Bailey flopped on the floor, squishing up a pillow to prop herself on. "Besides what do brains look like?"

"You're right. I shouldn't lump all guys together but what if we did a kind of mini-makeover on you just to draw a little more attention to you?"

"You mean more attention than I got for spilling salsa all down the front of Trevor? How about if we put me in the witness protection program and see if they'll give me a new face and a new identity."

"Stop. You worry too much about things. That was Friday. By tomorrow, a whole new week will have been started and everyone will have forgotten."

"You think Trevor will have forgotten?"

"Trevor was there. He knew it was an accident."

"He may know it's an accident—I hope he does anyway—but he'll still see me as a klutzy ditz. I wish I could be confident and graceful."

"That's what I'm talking about," Jenn said.

"Okay," Bailey said. "I guess a makeover can't hurt, right?"

They both headed for Jenn's bedroom. Jenn had a knack with clothes, hair, and makeup. Back in junior high, it was Jenn who helped Bailey learn to style her own hair. Every time Bailey went to pick out new glasses, her mom let her bring Jenn along. As Mom always said, the girl had an eye for it.

It was definitely a knack. Bailey could try on pair after pair of jeans, not being able to see much difference. If she took Jenn along, her friend would talk about fit, proportion, and movement. And could she ever spot a bargain. It's probably why she always looked so good. No amount of money could make up for that sense of style.

"I'm lucky to have you for a friend," Bailey said as she sat down on the edge of Jenn's bed.

"What brought that up?" Jenn asked. "Not that I'll argue with you."

"How many people would put so much energy into trying to make their friend better?"

"That's what we've always done for each other. This is my area of expertise," she said, emphasizing each syllable of the word. "I'm good at social things and even better at makeup and clothes. But you, how many times have you dragged my nose into a calculus book?" She shrugged. "This is what friends are for."

"Okay, I'm putty in your hands."

Jenn started with makeup. "For the most part your makeup is good. I like the lip gloss you've been using. Because your hair is such a strong color, I think we should use a tiny bit of color over your cheeks. Let's try it."

"Are you saying my hair is too strong?" She knew that her hair fell somewhere between carrot and an auburn. There was nothing subtle about it.

"Are you kidding? We are trying to make you stand out. Your hair takes us halfway there already. It's just that you don't get enough mileage out of it."

Bailey looked in the mirror. Maybe she shouldn't always pull it back in a ponytail, but it was so quick and kept it out of her face.

When Jenn finished with makeup, she left Bailey's glasses off. "For this week only, can you leave your glasses in your backpack until you get into class?"

"You don't like my glasses?"

"Of course I do. I helped pick them out, but I'm experimenting with a new look for you." She got a hand mirror and brought it close so Bailey could see without her glasses. "See how dreamy your eyes look?"

"I think so." Bailey squinted.

"I'd like to go for a softer look—not so brainy."

"How do I look brainy?"

"I didn't mean it negatively, it's just that you seem so 'in charge.' Could it be that guys are put off?"

"I don't think Trevor was put off until I showered him in salsa."

"Knock, knock." Luke stuck his head in the door. "It sounds like way too much fun in here. Can I join?"

"Only if you'd like me to give you a makeover," Jenn said.

"What are you doing to poor Bailey?" he asked.

Bailey squinted at the mirror. "What? Are you doing something weird, Jenn?"

Luke laughed. "No, I mean this whole reinvention thing. I see it every day on the set at *Dating Do-Over.* I'm feeling like it's an epidemic."

"We're just trying out a newer, dreamier look for Bailey. See? I want her to leave her glasses off so those blue eyes of hers stand out. What do you think?"

"Don't you wear your glasses so you can see?" Luke looked into the mirror at Bailey.

"I'm very nearsighted."

"Well, I wouldn't give up glasses just to show off eye makeup. Besides, Jenn, I noticed Bailey's blue eyes long ago, in spite of glasses."

That surprised Bailey. Luke had noticed her eyes? She knew he was a good listener and they'd often been together in a small group at church, but her eyes?

"You're such a guy with a guy's point of view," Jenn said.

"But isn't that the point—getting a guy's opinion?"

"Why don't you go tell Mom she needs you?"

"Okay, I can see when I'm not wanted. You be careful, Bailey. My sister used to cut her doll's hair right down to the roots. She has a whole basket of nub-headed Barbies."

Jenn gave him that look, and he grinned as he backed out the door.

"Forget what he said. I want you to try to go without glasses between classes, just for this week." Jenn got out her mousse, curling iron, and hairspray. "Now for your hair."

She took some mousse and scrunched it into Bailey's hair, then blew it dry while fluffing it up. "See how I'm doing this? I want to give you some volume—to let your curls free."

"And I need to do this at home, before school?" Bailey was already rushed to help get the girls dressed while Mom cooked breakfast and to still get herself together and out the door.

"For one week. Can you give me one week?"

"I'll try."

After the dryer, Jenn took sections of Bailey's hair and wound each one on her curling iron. With a whole head of bouncy curls, Bailey wondered if she looked as much like Medusa as she felt.

"Now, those curls will soften and settle down, but you'll still have the movement and volume." Jenn poked and pulled at the curls arranging them and then rearranging them. "Do you think you can do this?"

Bailey put on her glasses and looked into the mirror. "I think so."

"And then when you start another round of interviews for our poll, you'll feel confident."

"There's no way I can do the poll without my glasses." Bailey didn't need another thing to worry about.

"You're nearsighted. Sure you can."

Bailey groaned. "I don't want to be negative, Jenn, but I have trouble feeling confident when I can't see. I'll give it a try tomorrow, but . . ."

"Okay, fair enough." Jenn sat beside her on the bed. "Have you thought any more about possible prom dates?"

"I haven't had time with this whole plan of yours."

"Maybe that's good. It takes some of the pressure off." Jenn stood up and went over to open her closet doors. "I need to start looking for my dress, but I was hoping to be able to do it together."

"What was that about taking off pressure?"

"But all you have to do is decide you are going—date or not—and we can start."

There was no stopping Jenn. Bailey knew that long ago. "Give me a couple weeks. I'll try hard to decide by the first meeting of the decorating committee. By then I'll have taken time to look around at church for some unsuspecting guy."

"Oh stop. You know what I mean. We just need some time to plan for our clothes and make arrangements." Jenn started picking up some of the makeup. "But you're right. It's a good idea to wait 'til the theme is set. We may want to plan our clothes around the theme."

Bailey pulled her things together and got out the car keys. "Have you heard if Trevor has a date yet?"

"No, not a single word about it. Have you noticed,

though, how that group of junior girls hangs around him? It makes me think he's still unattached and they're all sticking close, especially Sienna, just in case."

"I hadn't thought of that. They were crowded around on Friday when . . . well you know."

"Did he say anything about the prom when you interviewed him?" Jenn wound the cord around her blow dryer.

"I never got that far."

"Be sure to finish with him."

Bailey laughed. "Oh, I'm guessing he's already finished with me."

"I don't know," Jenn said, pausing for a minute. "He seems different lately somehow. Maybe quieter?"

"I haven't noticed, but maybe I've been so focused on prom, I haven't paid attention." Bailey shook her head. "What is wrong with me? Did you hear that? Focused on prom? I don't think I like what this quest for a prom date is doing to me."

"You stop," Jenn said, poking her friend. "It's natural to try to make the most of your senior year. Don't start beating yourself up. You are always sensitive to other people. If you haven't noticed anything, it's probably not there."

Bailey didn't know what to say. "I should get going, especially if I'm going to do makeup, hair, and clothes for tomorrow. I need to get to bed early since I'll need to get up at oh-dark-hundred."

"Yikes. We didn't talk clothes."

"Like we need to. You've been shopping with me for nearly everything in my closet. Each time I go to reach for something, I hear you telling what to wear with it." Bailey laughed. "Your voice is my little style conscience."

Bailey managed to pull off a close facsimile of Jenn's makeover. She wore a lime fitted tee and the pair of jeans that Jenn liked best. She even put in a pair of earrings. This was as good as it gets.

She left early so she could try to get a couple of interviews done before class. Jenn had already put so much effort into this plan that Bailey decided to give it 100 percent.

As soon as she got to school, she took her glasses off and tucked the case into her backpack. She could see things close in front of her, but the whole world looked fuzzy beyond that. As she walked into the cafeteria, she saw a group of guys. How could she tell who was who?

"Hey, Bailey."

She recognized the shape and the voice of Gary from her calculus class.

"Hi, Gary. Would you have a few minutes to answer some questions for my Econ project?"

"Are you kidding? I heard about your questions."

"Oh come on, Gary." Bailey couldn't believe she was pressing him. Maybe it was easier to talk to guys when you couldn't really see them. "If you're talking about Trevor, that was an accident."

"Oh, all right. You have helped me in Calculus." He made room for her at his table as a few of the guys left. "You look different."

Good. At least someone noticed. "How do I look different?" Bailey couldn't believe she asked. It was almost like flirting. Too bad Gary was an old friend. An old friend with a girlfriend.

"I don't know. Your hair? Your clothes? Something. You look nice."

"Thanks." Bailey could feel herself smiling. "Okay, let's get started. Have you ever been out on a date?"

"Yep."

Before she could write his answer, someone bumped into her hard and her pencil ran across the questionnaire.

"Oh, did I do that?" Bailey recognized the fake-sweet voice as one of the girls who hung with Trevor. Was it Sienna?

"You know you did," Gary said with a puzzled look on his face. "You need to be careful. There's plenty of room to walk between the benches. You don't have to be bumping into those of us at the tables. What if Bailey had a hot chocolate in her hand?"

"Well, it would have been as much of an accident as Bailey's salsa spill."

Bailey stood up to leave. "Gary, why don't we finish this in Calculus? We usually get done early."

Gary agreed and Bailey gathered her things together and left. She didn't want to make a scene but that incident made no sense. Why would a girl she hardly knew get involved in something that had nothing to do with her?

"What was that about?"

"Jenn?" Bailey could tell by the muzzy outline and the voice.

"Yes. By the way, you look great today."

"Thanks. I have no idea what that was about. I think it was Sienna, Trevor's friend. She came up behind me and bumped into me. Weird. Rather than stay around and exchange words with her, I just left."

"Well, let's not lose any time. You need to find someone else to interview."

"Could you identify someone for me and point me in their direction?"

"Oh c'mon. Your eyesight is not that bad."

"It's not?"

"Okay. Head over to Jordan at two o'clock."

Bailey could make him out somewhat and went over and did a complete interview before the bell rang. It felt good to finally get a questionnaire finished. As she walked to class, she took her glasses out of her case and put them on. Now she felt even better.

By the time lunch came, she was ready to do a couple more interviews. She picked a junior guy who seemed honored by her asking. It went well and she found him easy to talk to. As she finished up, Jenn came alongside her.

"Your glasses," she whispered.

"What?"

She got closer. "You're wearing your glasses."

Oops. Bailey took off her glasses and put them in the case inside her backpack.

"Bailey?"

She turned around to see Trevor.

"Luke tells me you're feeling awful about the accident on Friday. At first I thought the guys had gotten you to do their dirty work, but I realized that was ridiculous before I'd even blotted the gunk off my shirt."

"Thanks, Trevor. I'll admit I was worried that you thought I'd done it on purpose."

"We've gotten to know each other in class this year. I should have known better."

Bailey didn't know what to say.

"Did the stains come out of your clothes?" he asked.

"Yes. Yours?"

"Uh huh." He held his hands out to the side to show off the front of his shirt. "I wore the same shirt so you could see no harm was done. My mom's a wonder with prewash." He shifted weight from one foot to another. "Would you like me to finish your questionnaire?"

"Yes. Thank you." She put her backpack down and fumbled in it to get her clipboard back out.

"I'm heading off now," Jenn said.

Bailey hadn't remembered she was there. "Bye, Jenn. Catch you later." She turned to Trevor. "Shall we sit down?"

They slid into an empty bench. Bailey wished she could see well enough to see if Trevor's friends were nearby. She still felt shaken by the incident with Sienna. "Okay, here's your sheet. Let's see . . . I was asking you what kind of date you prefer: informal with a group of kids—a movie or event date; or a formal date—like a prom?"

"I don't know. Prom would be special—something you remember forever, but I also like to just go out with a whole group or even to get together to watch football."

"So which do you prefer?"

"I'll just say prom, since it stands out. Plus I like to get dressed up once in a while."

"You're the first guy who's picked prom. I guess I shouldn't tell you that until we get all the data in, but . . ." Bailey almost felt comfortable talking with Trevor this time. "Are you planning to go to the prom?" She couldn't believe she asked that.

"I don't know. I can't decide. Things are—"

"Trevor, what are you doing?" It was Sienna with a group of girls. "You must like to live dangerously."

"Can't you see I'm busy, Sienna?" His voice seemed flat.

"Well, I'd watch out for her. She's clumsy and you've already been her victim once."

Trevor ignored her. "You look different today, Bailey. Did you get contacts?"

Bailey laughed. She'd have to give this one to Jenn. "No, I just took off my glasses . . . giving my eyes a rest. Shall we finish?"

She asked the rest of the questions but never managed to get back to the prom question. It didn't matter. This went well, and it felt as if their friendship had opened up. "Thanks so much for helping us with the poll." She packed up, slid her arms into her backpack, and turned to get out of the bench. As she swung her leg over the bench, her backpack was jerked hard, throwing her off balance. She felt herself falling backward. Her right leg jerked upward trying to counterbalance, and she could feel it connect hard with something.

Trevor reached out and grabbed her before her head could hit the floor. "What happened?"

"I don't know," she said, trying to catch a breath. Her heart pounded so hard she could barely breathe. "I felt my backpack jerk back. I must have caught it on something . . . but what?" She looked around. There was nothing it could have hooked on. Somebody must have grabbed it. Could it have been an accident? Or maybe someone walked by and accidentally caught it on something? But they would have stopped to help catch her, wouldn't they?

Trevor's eyes narrowed as he looked beyond her.

"Are you all right?" he asked, rubbing his jaw. A large red area had appeared there.

"I'm fine." Without thinking, she touched his jaw. "Look at this. I'm so sorry. My foot hit you." He wasn't safe with her around. "That's going to be a huge bruise."

"Don't worry about it." He stood up. "I need to go."

She didn't say anything more. All the ease of their earlier talk had vanished. How she wished she'd worn her glasses so she could have seen it coming. It was one thing to be clumsy, but to be left defenseless for the sake of vanity was just plain foolish.

RealTV

Chatter Challenged

4

Wednesday, April 6th

To: AskAngela@MetroGirlZine
From: ChatterChallenged@Wazoo.com

Dear Ask Angela,

    Okay, so u are never going to answer. U probably get thousands of e-mails so I'm not going to worry about u thinking I'm a stalker or something; I'm just going to keep writing. It's a break from my diary. Just in case u read this, I'm the one who's on a mission to find a prom date . . . except I keep getting sidetracked.

What is it that makes one girl get asked over and over while another never gets asked once? Is it looks? I don't think so. Most people see me as reasonably good-looking. My friend even did a mini-makeover on me that attracted attention. She says the problem might be conversation. What do you think?

Chatter Challenged

❋   ❋   ❋

Bailey pressed the "send" button. How she wished she could get an answer once and for all. Jenn's newest installment in her Bailey-reinvention plan included learning to giggle and chatter. Bailey hated those words. Why not an honest laugh and good conversation?

"Are you sitting here brooding?" Jenn asked coming into the room with one of the M&Ms on each hand. "Look what I found on my way up to your room."

"Pway, Bay-we?" Madeline asked.

"There's no time to play. You need to get dressed, and I need to get ready for school." She shooed the girls out of her room and called down to her mother, "Mom, can you dress the girls this morning? Jenn is here."

She came back into the room after her mom took the girls. "I take it you are here with the next install-ment of the plan."

"Snap." This was Jenn's new word. It seemed to mean a resounding yes. "You did a great job with the poll, but that was only an exercise—more like school-work than spontaneous conversation."

"You've got to admit it helped us get our Econ assignment done."

"And that's not a bad thing. We're the first ones finished." Jenn slipped off her shoes and plopped down on Bailey's bed, resting her stocking feet against the headboard. "Okay, next phase . . ."

"Oh, Jenn, I'm about ready to throw in the towel. Each thing I've tried ended in some kind of catastrophe. Seeing Trevor's jaw all black-and-blue from being kicked in the face by me was the absolute worst."

"It wasn't your fault and you know it."

She did know it. The more she thought about it, the more she realized that someone staged that accident. She suspected Sienna because of the earlier incident when she interviewed Gary, but she had no idea what Sienna had against her. Could it be that she sensed Bailey's interest in Trevor and she didn't want competition? That seemed way far-fetched.

"You are obsessing again. We need to launch the next task to take your mind off this."

"Okay, I give." Besides, Bailey wanted to get downstairs to breakfast. "What's the assignment, boss?"

"We're going to explore a whole new kind of communication—girlie chatter, giggles, and passing notes." Jenn sat up and put her hands on her hips. "It's just another way to become more at ease with communication."

"You've got to be kidding. Guys don't like chatter, giggles, and notes." This challenge made no sense at all.

"They say they don't, but haven't you seen guys around the giggly girls? Look at the group that hangs around Trevor. They're forever passing notes and chattering." Jenn stood up and walked to the window. "Not all guys like it, that's for sure. Luke is always complaining about what he calls insipid chatter, but most guys think it's cute."

"Luke doesn't like it?" As Bailey had come to know Luke a little better, she realized that he didn't seem to worry about being one of the crowd. She couldn't help admiring his individuality.

"No, but he can be an old stick. Besides, you don't want to date Luke; you want to catch the eye of someone who's fun."

Bailey decided not to argue the point. Luke may not be into all the stuff—whatever it was—that went into flirting, but he was no old stick.

"Learning to take part in lighthearted conversation is important," Jenn continued. "It's the first step. The poll gave you structure. Now it's time to do some free-form conversation."

It didn't pay to protest. Jenn was doing this for Bailey's good. "So what do you want me to do?"

Jenn held up her hand. "First." She raised a finger. "I want you to figure out a way to engage in some purely silly talk in front of a guy or two."

Bailey shut her eyes.

"Second . . ." Up went the next finger. "I want you to giggle a few times today."

"I don't even know how to giggle. I mean how do you make that sound, anyway?"

"I'm not going to let you sidetrack me." Jenn raised the third finger. "And I want you pass a silly note to a guy in class—three tasks."

"But isn't it against most class rules to pass notes?"

"You just have to do it before or after class—before the teacher opens her mouth or after she closes the book."

"That's all, huh?" Bailey breathed in deeply and let it out in a sigh. "C'mon. We better get going or the only note I'll be needing will be a tardy excuse."

As the girls walked to school, Bailey wondered how she'd manage this one. Jenn was right about one thing. Doing these tasks kept her mind off the prom. True, she was no closer to a date now than she was when she started, but it felt as if she was doing something anyway.

How to giggle? She didn't know if she could be enough of an actress. Giggling would not come naturally. She wanted to get the giggling part out of the way first thing. If Jenn was right and reinventing herself was a first step to finding a prom date, at least she planned to take that step.

Halfway to school, Luke and Jace caught up with them.

"Where'd you go this morning, Jenn?" Luke asked.

"We had more planning to do so I went over to Bailey's."

"Uh, oh, Jace." Luke smiled. "More planning."

Bailey tried to giggle. It came out more like a cackle.

"Are you getting a cough?" Jace asked.

Jenn started laughing in earnest. "She's trying to learn to giggle."

"That's a giggle?" Luke asked. "Why would you want to giggle anyway?"

"It's a feminine thing. Lighthearted and all that," Jenn answered.

Luke mimicked the sound Bailey had made. It sounded like a toy machine gun. Both Bailey and Jenn cracked up at the sound. They couldn't stop.

"What are you girls giggling about?" Gary came up behind them. "It sounds like you're having fun."

They laughed even harder. Between gasps Bailey said, "Cross that off my list. Gary used the word 'giggle.' I'm finished with that challenge."

"Well, I, for one, am glad that you don't need to ever attempt a giggle again," Luke said. "I don't think I can take it."

Both girls started laughing all over again.

"I'd like to be around when Bailey has to chatter," Jace said. "It should be as good as her giggle."

"Oh, stop it," Jenn said, trying to catch her breath. "You guys have no appreciation for the true feminine mystique."

They continued to laugh most of the way to school.

Bailey wanted to get the second challenge out of the way as early as she could, so she penned a note to send to Trevor in second period. It read: *Dear Trevor, I'm feeling terrible about the other day. I'm still embarrassed about leaving a mark on your face. Thank you for keeping me from ending up on the floor. Next time I'll be more careful. Bailey.*

There. That should work. It qualified as a note even though it was little more than a formal apology. As soon as he came in and sat down, she leaned over to Maree, who sat in the next chair, and whispered, "Would you pass this note to Trevor, please?"

Maree took the note but got distracted and didn't pass it on immediately. Bailey kept looking at the note waving in Maree's hand as she talked. It seemed like forever, but when she finally finished her conversation she passed the note on to another girl.

Bailey couldn't take her eyes from the note. She watched it move from hand to hand until it got to the girl who sat next to Trevor. Bailey hated this. Could anyone consider this fun?

As the girl turned to pass the note to Trevor, a friend of Sienna's stood up from the other side of Trevor and grabbed the note from the girl's hand. She smiled at Bailey as she turned toward the teacher who'd just come into the room.

"Ms. Barnard, this note is floating around out here. It's probably for you."

No! This was not the way it was supposed to work. Hadn't Jenn called it lighthearted?

The teacher took the note. "As you know, whenever anyone passes a note in class, we read it out loud."

No! Please, no. Bailey couldn't believe this.

"Dear Trevor," Ms. Barnard read. "I'm feeling terrible about the other day. I'm still embarrassed about leaving a mark on your face." Ms. Barnard seemed embarrassed.

Someone in the back of class hooted.

"I don't know what kind of mark you're referring to, Ms. Tollefson, but I don't think we need hear any more of this. Will you please see me after class?"

Bailey put her head down. What did Ms. Barnard think she meant? She didn't even want to consider. What must Trevor be thinking? She didn't know how she'd make it through an entire period. Why couldn't the floor open up and swallow her whole?

They must have covered subject matter of some kind in the class, but if Ms. Barnard would have popped a quiz, Bailey knew she would have earned her first-ever failing grade. She couldn't think of a single thing except her humiliation. She kept feeling the heat of shame creep up her neck.

Just before class ended a note was slipped onto her

desk. It read: *Don't sweat it, Bailey. I knew what you meant. Trevor.*

She looked over at Trevor and tried to smile her thanks.

By the time class was over, she was ready to face Ms. Barnard and explain the whole thing.

"I'm sorry for passing a note, Ms. Barnard, but I started it way before class and it sort of stalled along the way."

"I'll admit I was surprised, Bailey. And I read the meaning wrong until I saw the bruise on Trevor's face. I'm sorry about that part. What happened?"

"Someone knocked me off my seat in the cafeteria, and I managed to kick Trevor in the jaw trying to get my balance. It was not my finest moment."

"Someone knocked you off? Who?"

"I don't know for sure. I wasn't wearing my glasses."

"It could have ended up a lot worse than Trevor's bruise." Ms. Barnard seemed more upset about the cafeteria incident than about the note. "If you find out that someone did this as a prank or, even worse, deliberately, you need to take this situation to the principal."

Bailey agreed and thanked her teacher for understanding. Straightening the note mess out had taken so long she had to run to her next class. As soon as she sat down, Jenn wanted to know what happened.

"I passed the note, but it got handed to the teacher and I very nearly died of embarrassment." Bailey stopped whispering as the teacher got up but then she stepped out of the room and Bailey continued. "My note didn't make it, but Trevor passed one to me, so I can cross that one off the list, too." She sighed. "I never want to do that again."

"So you only have one part of this challenge left, right?"

Bailey gave Jenn her best are-you-kidding look as the teacher came back into the room. One more challenge. Okay, she'd do it. She was no quitter.

Jenn smiled as if she knew that Bailey would do it.

Chatter. That was it. She'd probably be as successful at chatter as she was at giggling and passing notes. This reinventing herself was hard work. She wanted to change, but all of this felt so strange.

When the bell rang for lunch, she determined to get it over with as soon as she could. Chatter. Light chatter, in fact. What could she chatter about?

Luke stood with Trevor and a group of friends. Might as well join them.

"Hey, Bailey," Luke said. "Heard you got busted for passing notes."

"Don't torture her," Trevor said. "She's had a rough few encounters with me lately. I'm surprised she's not running when she sees me."

Light chatter. "You're worth every wound," Bailey said, trying for a light note.

Trevor looked surprised, but not as surprised as Luke. He looked stunned for a moment and then he smiled and nodded.

Bailey knew Luke had figured out that this was part of her makeover. She laughed again. She didn't have the nerve to try for a giggle, but the laugh was light. "Trevor, are you playing baseball during Friday's game?" *Keep it going.* "I just love baseball." *There.*

"Yes, I'm playing. I didn't know you were a fan of the game. Why don't you come?"

"I'd love to, especially if I can watch you play."

Bailey hated the way that sounded, but she smiled. She figured it should be enough to fulfill the chatter requirement.

Luke smirked as he caught her eye.

Before another disaster could take place, Bailey excused herself to get into the lunch line where Jenn joined her.

"Okay, cross number three off your list," Bailey said. "I chattered. I told Trevor that I liked baseball, and he invited me to his game Friday."

"You're kidding! You talked baseball? I didn't know you even knew what a baseball looked like."

"I don't. I used up the sum total of my sports knowledge in our conversation. Somehow I remembered that the game he plays this time of year is baseball. Amazing, huh?"

"Since you told him you like baseball how do you plan to hide the fact that you know absolutely nothing about the game?"

Bailey hadn't thought about that.

RealTV

No Runs, No Hits, Just Errors

5

Friday, April 8th

To: AskAngela@MetroGirlZine
From: YoureOut@Wazoo.com

Dear Ask Angela,

Me again. This all started out as a quest for a prom date. The further I go, the more complicated this whole thing gets. I mean I've been humiliated in the cafeteria and embarrassed in front of the whole class—and both times in front of the guy I'd hoped would ask me to the prom. Oh, yeah, I managed to kick him in the jaw leaving him black-and-blue—don't ask.

If u didn't know me, you'd probably say that it's time for things to turn around, but let me tell you about the baseball game . . .

❋   ❋   ❋

Bailey interweaved her fingers and gave her knuckles a crack. *Good thing Mom isn't here to hear that pop.* It seemed like a great opportunity when Trevor asked her to go to his baseball game. It was almost like a predate.

She told him she loved baseball—that's where she went off track. The truth is she wished she loved baseball since he played baseball, but she didn't know a single thing about the game. She'd played softball in PE but hadn't paid all that much attention to it.

She would not worry, though. It was Wednesday when she decided to go. That gave her forty-eight hours to cram sports info into her brain. Study was something she did best. She was nothing if not a good student. And as long as she was cramming, she decided to do football and basketball as well since Trevor also liked those.

By the time Friday came her mind swam with terms. Four quarters in a game. Overtime. Referees. Umpires. Foul ball. Penalty. Errors. She was as ready as she could be.

"Are you sure you want me to come?" Jenn asked her after school. "I don't want to be in the way."

"Please come. Trevor is going to be playing, and I don't want to be left alone with his loyal fans like Sienna."

"Luke always catches the game unless he has to work. He usually doesn't work on Fridays unless filming for the week runs late. He could protect you."

"Do you think I need protecting?" It was true— Sienna seemed to have developed a strong dislike for her, but Bailey figured it would blow over. *Could Sienna be crushing on Trevor? If they were going out, wouldn't he have said something during the questionnaire? And wouldn't he have asked her to the prom?*

"Probably not, but that incident with your backpack was weird. Anyway, if you want me to join you, I'll be happy to come. It'll be fun to watch Trevor play in front of you."

They stowed their stuff in their lockers and walked out to the baseball field. "I'm glad we're the home team," Bailey said. "We've got home team advantage."

"Wow. I'm impressed. You did bone up on sports, didn't you?"

"I read so much, it's all swirling in my mind. I'm not going to make any comments on special teams or strategies or any of the advanced stuff. I need to stay generic."

"Are you sure you don't want to just confess that you are a baseball newbie?" Jenn kicked a stone out of the path.

"I thought about that, but I already made it sound like I lived for baseball. *Metro Girl Magazine* said it's important to be interested in what your guy's interested in." Bailey walked along without saying anything until they got closer to the field. "I mean it isn't exactly a lie since I've been thinking of little else other than the game since I first thought about Trevor playing baseball."

Jenn didn't say anything.

As they climbed onto the bleachers, Bailey caught sight of Trevor warming up on the field. He was playing outfield. Which spot was that? Left field? Right field? It all depended if they named the positions while standing out in the field or sitting on the bleachers.

There could be no asking Jenn in private because as Bailey looked up she saw Sienna and her entourage moving up the bleacher steps, talking and laughing. When Sienna spotted Bailey, her whole face changed, narrowing somehow. She turned toward one of the girls and whispered something behind a cupped hand. They turned into the row one step above Bailey and side-stepped down until she bumped and jostled her way to a seat right behind them.

"Ouch!" Something hit Bailey sharply on the back of her head.

"My bad," Sienna said, giggling. "That thermos is just too big."

Bailey thought about getting up and finding a different spot, but that would look weird. Besides, Trevor had looked up and spotted her before the others even sat down. If she moved, they might miss each other.

Just as the umpire came out to the plate and leaned over and swept it off with a little broom, Luke sat down beside her. "I didn't know you liked baseball."

Jenn laughed and whispered, "Neither did she until Wednesday."

Bailey gave Jenn a look. "I'm actually a student of the game."

Jenn snorted.

"I wish the referee would blow his whistle and sound the 'play ball' so I could watch baseball instead of having to take this abuse." Bailey smiled. There. She'd used some of her terminology.

Luke threw his head back and laughed. "Forgive me for doubting you. You are definitely a student of base-ball."

"What?" Bailey heard the sarcasm in his voice. She hoped Sienna and her friends hadn't heard.

Luke came in close and whispered, "Baseball has umpires, not referees. And umpires do not use whistles. And I don't think they yell 'play ball' in high school in-tramural sports. But other than that, you're right. They do call the game baseball."

Bailey couldn't help herself. She laughed out loud. As she looked up, she saw Trevor looking up into the stands right at her with a scowl on his face. Maybe he'd misunderstood Luke's closeness and her laugh. Oh well . . . nothing she could do now.

The umpire nodded toward the other team's coach, and the first batter came out.

Since Trevor was keeping one eye on the stands, she decided she'd better be enthusiastic. When the batter tipped the ball and sent it flying between the third base-man and the San Vincente bench, Bailey jumped up and yelled, "Offsides, offsides!"

Trevor looked up at her, a surprised look on his face.

"Um, Bay . . ." Luke could hardly keep from crying he laughed so hard. "Offsides is a football term. The usual term around baseball is foul ball."

Bailey sat back down. She wondered if she could slip away without being seen.

Sienna leaned forward. "Trevor mentioned you were quite the baseball fan. Could it be that you exaggerated a wee bit?"

Jenn turned around. "Can you please mind your own business?"

"My friends are my business. I have no idea why your friend started stalking Trevor, but I'm on to her. He may be clueless right now, but I'm not." She stood up and began a singsong chant, "Hey batter, batter, batter . . . Swing!"

Luke turned toward Bailey. "Would you like to find a more comfortable seat?"

Bailey sighed. Sienna might be antagonistic toward her, but the girl had a point. Bailey had focused in on Trevor recently. She hadn't been part of his group or even built a friendship first. Maybe she and Jenn would be just as suspicious if someone made a similar project out of Luke. "No," she said, leaning toward Luke. "I deserved that."

Luke looked hard at her, but said no more. They continued to watch the game.

As Bailey watched, she couldn't help feeling bad. While the rest of the home fans were glued to the close game, she prayed silently. *Lord, please forgive me. I've been so focused on this goal that I even lied about knowing baseball. What is wrong with me?*

Bailey decided she'd come clean with Trevor the first chance she got. Deception didn't feel good at all. She had always tried to be straightforward and honest. Now, she'd been caught in a lie in front of friends and enemies.

When Sienna and her friends went down to the snack bar, Bailey turned to Luke. "Will you forgive me for lying about sports? And you, too, Jenn . . . will you forgive me? I don't know what made me say the things I said, but I don't like what's happening to me."

"Of course I forgive you," Jenn said. "It was really more like a funny joke . . . like a game, than an outright lie."

"But I know what you're saying, Bay," Luke said, draping an arm around her. "Sometimes we start out playacting, but before long it turns into something more." He pulled back his arm. "Yikes, I'm beginning to sound like an old uncle or something. Ignore me."

"No, you make sense."

"Well, I like it that you are sensitive enough to call it a lie."

"Now I have to be honest with Trevor." She looked down on the field where he stood looking up at her. Was he scowling because he'd already realized she was a phony?

The noisy group, led by Sienna, came back to their seats, laden with snacks. For the rest of the game Bailey watched the action to the accompaniment of their crunching and smacking. It was a close game, but San Vincente managed to pull out ahead in the last inning. When they won, Bailey stood and cheered with the rest of them.

"Trevor!" Sienna yelled right into Bailey's left ear. "We'll meet you in the parking lot."

Trevor waved from the field. "No, I'm coming up before I shower."

Bailey wondered if she should slip out and catch him later, but he was already making his way up, two steps at a time.

"Great game, Trev," Sienna said as Trevor walked toward where Luke sat. She jumped down to their row to intercept Trevor before he reached where they were sitting.

"Thanks, Sienna." Trevor stepped down to the row below them, sidestepping Sienna's block. He turned to look at Bailey. "So what did you think of the game?" He wasn't smiling.

"Which game?" Sienna interrupted. "Bailey seemed to think it was football season."

"I better get going," Bailey said. She could feel the heat creeping up her face. "Actually, though, Sienna's right. I led you to believe I'm a baseball enthusiast." She inhaled deeply, fortifying herself. "I'm gonna have to ask you to forgive me for that. I wasn't being honest. I'm new to the game, but today was a great initiation for me." She couldn't believe she was talking so openly to Trevor . . . and in front of a hostile audience. "You guys played great."

"Thanks." He seemed uncomfortable. "I figured you weren't really a baseball fan when you yelled 'offsides.'" Frown lines etched the space between his eyebrows. "I don't know why you pretended an interest in the first place."

"Maybe she just wanted to show an interest in what interested you," Luke said.

Trevor ignored Luke and looked at Bailey. "Why would you do that?"

Bailey couldn't answer. So much for conversation.

Trevor shook his head in confusion. "I don't get you. I saw Luke with his arm around you and whispering in your ear, and yet . . ." He shrugged. "I just don't get it."

He looked over at Sienna. "How about if you guys wait for me to shower, and then we'll grab a Coke."

Sienna smiled. "Sure, Trev."

When they had left, Luke turned to Bailey. "I'm so sorry, Bailey. He totally misunderstood."

"No, he may have misunderstood us, but he was right about me. I don't even recognize myself." She didn't wait for Jenn and Luke as she walked down the bleachers and headed toward her locker.

"Don't you want to get something to drink, Bailey, before you go home?" Jenn hurried to catch up with her.

"No, but thanks. I just need to go do some thinking."

"Please don't go," Jenn said. "I'm the one who pushed you into this. I feel awful."

"No, it's not your plan that's to blame. In fact, I got some good practice with conversation and having fun in a group. I'm the one responsible for pretending to be something I'm not." She opened her locker and took out the books she'd need for the weekend. "I'll call you tonight. I'm really okay—not going off the deep end or anything."

"Okay, but I'll call you if I don't hear." Jenn yelled to her brother over at his locker, "Wait up, Luke. I'll walk home with you."

RealTV

Trapped in Tinseltown

6

Friday, April 15th

To: AskAngela@MetroGirlZine
From: TrappedinTinseltown@Wazoo.com

Dear Ask Angela,
    It's been a whole week since I've written.
U must be thinking my life has turned around
and I'm busy searching for the perfect prom
dress. U would be way wrong. Nothing has
changed. If u have any advice for me, send it

on. Please. Otherwise, I'll sign off forever and go back to my faithful diary.

Oh yes, I've been drafted for the prom decorating committee. It's déjà vu all over again. Our theme—since we are so near the movie capitol of the world—is Tinseltown.

So, unless you come up with some great advice, I remain . . .

Trapped in Tinseltown

✺   ✺   ✺

Bailey hit the "send" button and took out her diary. She looked at her blank list of three guys. No one, no one, and no one. Looks like she got her wish. She would attend the prom with her first choice—no one.

Good thing Jenn wasn't here to accuse her of obsessing. She could obsess all she wanted. At least until it was time to leave for school. Her senior year was fast drawing to a close. She'd wanted so badly to throw herself into every single activity—to live this year to the fullest. For the most part, she'd done it. Except for prom. But it loomed large these days.

She'd even done her best to reinvent herself. And failed miserably. Since the game last Friday, Trevor seemed to be ignoring her big time.

"Hey, Princess," said Dad as he stuck his head in the door. "Are you coming down for breakfast? Mom cooked French toast."

"French toast? On a school day?" Her mom taught at the same daycare and preschool the M&Ms attended and mornings were usually a big rush.

"Your mom's been realizing that if you go away to

college next year our days of rushed mornings together will be coming to a close. I think she wants to draw these days out."

"You're going to make me cry, Dad."

"Don't cry. Come down and eat with us instead. I don't mind Mom feeling nostalgic if it means her famous French toast, do you?"

Bailey laughed. Ever since she was a baby, Dad could always tease her out of a mood.

As they walked downstairs, Bailey said, "I will never ever understand boys."

"I thought it was always men who said that. I mean about women."

"Whatever," Bailey sighed. "Girls are easy compared to guys."

Mom looked up with a spatula in her hand. "What do you mean, 'girls are easy'?"

"We're talking about understanding the opposite sex," Dad said, getting Mallory and Madeline up to the table.

"What don't you understand about boys, Bailey?" Mom asked. "Or is it one boy in particular?"

Bailey usually didn't talk about guys with her parents. It felt awkward, but she was getting desperate. "It is one guy. We've been in class together all year and become friends. Not outside of school but in class."

Mom brought the plates to the table. "Hold that thought. Let's stop and say grace, so the girls can get started. They take so long to eat."

Dad prayed and then helped the girls pour syrup on their French toast.

"So," Mom said as she poured coffee into Dad's cup, "what confuses you about this boy who's become your friend?"

"Boyfriend?" Mallory said trying out the word. "Bailey has a boyfriend?"

"Bay-we boyfriend?" Madeline mimicked.

Bailey groaned.

"Eat, girls," Dad said in his no-nonsense voice.

"He's nice and I sort of wished he'd ask me to the prom." Bailey felt funny saying this to her parents.

"Does this boy have a name?" Dad asked.

"Trevor."

"Does he go to church?" Mom asked.

"Mom! I'm not going to marry him." What was it about Mom that she always zeroed in on the totally wrong thing? "In fact, I won't even be going to the prom with him."

Dad set down his fork and quirked that eyebrow of his. He didn't need to say anything. Bailey knew it meant he was listening.

"Jenn was trying to help me become more—I don't know—more friendly and fun. Better social skills, as my teacher would say."

"How did she do that?" Mom asked. Her eyes widened as she looked over at the girls. "Madeline, you're dripping syrup on your T-shirt!"

"She had me practice talking to guys, she helped me do my hair and makeup—you know, all the stuff I've been doing lately."

Dad nodded. "Like studying sports."

"Don't remind me," Bailey took a bite. Maybe the syrupy French toast would help her forget the bitter taste of the game last Friday. "Anyway, it somehow all went wrong. Over the last couple of weeks I spilled food on him, kicked him by accident, and embarrassed him in class."

"And that's why things went wrong?" Mom asked.

"No. That's the funny part. Even after all that, he still seemed open to me. It was when I pretended to love baseball that he pulled away."

"Because he doesn't love baseball?" Mom asked.

"No. He does." Bailey continued to take bites of her breakfast. It made conversation harder, but it tasted so good. "It's just that he found out I didn't really love baseball. Not that he seemed upset about that. Maybe it was because I pretended to be something I'm not."

"Hmmm," Dad said. It was always his invitation to keep talking.

"And he misunderstood something between Luke and me."

"Luke D'Silva?" Mom asked.

Bailey nodded. "He sat with me at the baseball game, and Trevor seemed to misunderstand."

"We know Luke's family from church," Mom said turning to Bailey's dad.

"Right," Dad said, food in his mouth. He continued chewing.

"Mom, you're getting off track. It's not about Luke. It's Trevor I don't understand."

"Want to know a secret, Princess?" Dad asked. "Trevor probably doesn't understand Trevor either." He took a napkin and wiped Madeline's mouth. "Big difference between boys and girls. Big."

"What?" Bailey wiped Mallory's mouth, but the napkin was no match for the sticky syrup.

"Girls think about things, talk about things, and keep working on them until they finally come to some understanding, right?"

"I think so," Bailey said.

"If something or someone's actions confuse you, you keep figuring it out, talking it out, and working it out until you make sense of it, right? In fact you get all your girlfriends working on the problem as well. A guy's not that way. If something confuses him, he may just leave it alone. He'll walk away from it rather than having to deal with it."

"That's true," Mom said. "Even now your dad will often just shake his head and walk away."

"Let's not get personal," Dad said, laughing. "I was talking generalities."

"Let's talk more generalities later," Mom said. "I need to get to work. Bailey, will you just gather the dishes and put them in the sink in some soapy water? I'll get them when I get home this afternoon."

Later, as Bailey walked to school, she thought about what her dad had said. Could it be true? Trevor had pulled back—no question. Did she confuse him? Maybe. Especially if he thought she was flirting with Luke. Well, the whole thing confused her as well. Even if Trevor decided to stay away from her, why hadn't he asked anyone to the prom? When she'd interviewed him, he was the only guy at school to pick prom as his ideal date. Weird.

"Wait up, Bailey," Jenn yelled from behind her.

Bailey stopped and waited for her friend to catch up. "I thought I was later than usual this morning."

"I didn't get all my Hollywood glamour photos together until this morning." Jenn had always been a film buff. She loved the glitz of old Hollywood, especially the days of the elegant black-and-white classics. She loved the theme of this year's prom. "You did remember about our first decorating meeting this afternoon, right?"

"I did, but I'm having a little bit of trouble getting excited about it."

Jenn didn't say anything.

As they walked, Bailey realized how selfish that was. Jenn was enthusiastic about the prom and excited about the theme. "I take that back," Bailey said. "Can't you tell me when I sound so whiny?"

"I wish you were going." Jenn sighed. "We're going to have fun decorating and we're going to make it the best ever, but it would be so much more fun if we were both going. Won't you please come with us?"

"I'll think about it, Jenn, but whether or not I come, I'm making one decision right here and now." She stopped walking. Trying for a look of great solemnity, she said, "From this moment, I decide to stop worrying about prom. I'm going to enjoy every moment of creating the best movie set a prom has ever seen."

"You go, girl!" Jenn said, laughing. "Happiness is a decision. How many times has Pastor John said that to us?"

"You know what would be cool?" Bailey put out her hands as if modeling on the runway. "If I go, we both could dress as 1930-something movie starlets."

Jenn stared off into the distance as if to picture those starlets. "Brilliant! You're a genius, Bay. I can see us now—with your red hair you can have the waves of a Greta Garbo. With my dark hair, I can do a Veronica Lake. We could go for the Hollywood lingerie-style gowns of satin. I think they were bias-cut, you know. That's what made them slide over the body and flare at the hemline." Jenn took a breath. "Can you imagine? No fashion era since then has been as elegant, plus our moms will like that they are tasteful."

"Tasteful?" Bailey had never thought of Hollywood and taste in the same breath.

"Truly. The dresses may have had V-necklines, but they were not all low cut like what you see today. Even though they skim the body, they were made of heavy silk satin and they flowed over it like liquid."

"Liquid, eh? You are getting into this, aren't you?" Bailey loved it when her friend got going. Jenn loved fashion design and often visited the secondhand shops on Melrose Avenue just for inspiration. Bailey trusted her sense of style. "It sounds dreamy, and I hate to bring you down to earth, but we need to keep walking or we'll miss school entirely."

"Okay. I can walk and talk."

Bailey laughed. "Not when you're designing, but I'll guide you. Come on."

"We could do black and white . . . no, that would be too stark . . . ivory and shades of gray and black. You could have the ivory dress since your skin is so delicate. I could pull off black. The guys could wear gray tuxes."

"Guys?"

"Well, assuming you get a date. I'll bet Luke could borrow some vintage tuxedos for our dates from the studio that *Dating Do-Over* uses. He says they've been around since the old Metro-Goldwyn-Mayer days, and they have a huge archive. Maybe we could even get our dresses there."

"Can you imagine?" Now Bailey was getting excited. "Do you think they'd allow it?"

"I don't know, but they really like Luke there. Maybe we'd have to pay something to insure the costumes, but, who knows?"

They were still talking about it when they got to

school. Bailey wished she were really going, but even if she never got asked, she needed to plan and plot with Jenn. That was half the fun.

"I meant to ask, are you going to Extra Innings tonight?" That was the name of their church's youth group. They called it Fifth Quarter during football season and Extra Innings in the spring.

"I planned to. Are you guys driving?"

"Luke probably will. Want us to pick you up?"

"Sure."

"Good. Let's talk at lunch about ideas for the decorations so we can be prepared for the meeting this afternoon."

The day sped by. It seemed as if juniors and seniors could talk of nothing else besides prom. Bailey was glad she'd made the decision to throw herself into it, no matter whether she'd go or not. Like Jenn had said, happiness is a decision.

"I've got sketches," Jenn said, patting her binder as they met at their lockers.

"How'd you have time to do those since lunch?" Bailey asked. They'd only come up with the ideas at noon.

"Luckily, we had a sub last period who let us do homework. I have all weekend to do homework so I used the time to sketch out our ideas."

They headed over to the cafeteria. Bailey couldn't believe she was part of another decorating stint for a prom she probably wouldn't attend. Oh, well.

"Hey, girls," Luke joined them in the courtyard. "You going to the meeting?"

"Uh huh. Are you going?"

"Yeah. Filming got finished yesterday so I'm a free man."

"Have you decided if you're going to the prom, Luke?" Jenn asked.

Bailey hadn't even thought about whether Luke was going or not.

"I don't know. You know how I feel about the whole dating scene. I keep thinking that if I ask anyone then it'll get all weird. You know . . ."

"You just wish I'd go with my brother, don't you, Luke?" Jenn said, punching him in the arm.

"It would make things easier. Then Jace could go with Bailey."

Bailey hated feeling like someone who needed to be fixed-up—like someone being passed around. "That's okay, I'm still not out of the running for a *real* date." Why did she snap like that? This prom pressure made her crazy.

Luke didn't say anything right away. "Sorry, Bay, I was just kidding."

"I know. I didn't mean to be so snappish."

"See?" Luke said. "Prom makes everyone cranky."

They went into the cafeteria and joined the others there. It was the same crowd who had been together on other events. Sienna and a couple of her friends were the only new volunteers.

The office had picked Ms. Barnard to advise the committee. "Welcome and thank you for volunteering. Some of you have done this before, and we especially appreciate that you are coming back for more of this craziness."

The kids laughed. There was no question—it could get plenty crazy.

"I need a volunteer to head the committee. Luke?"

"I'm not really sure I'll be able to attend prom, Ms.

Barnard, and with my work schedule I may not be as faithful as I'd like." The head of the decorating committee got a special recognition on prom night.

"Fair enough." Ms. Barnard looked around the room. "Trevor?"

"I'm not sure I'm coming either. I'll work hard, but with baseball . . . I mean we had no game today, so I could come here, but . . ."

"Jenn?"

"Sure. I'd love to be chairman."

Bailey smiled. Nothing subtle about Jenn.

"Kiss-up," Sienna whispered to her friends just loud enough that Bailey overheard.

"Why don't you take over, Jenn," Ms. Barnard said as she sat down. "I'm here in an advisory capacity—to see that you stay within budget and get what you need." She sat down and took out a notepad.

"All right," Jenn said, standing up. "Let's call this meeting to order. We are going to have the prom to end all proms, and we have exactly one month to accomplish it. The first thing I want to suggest is that we change the day of this meeting to Thursday afternoons." Jenn looked around the room. "Several of us have Fifth Inning on Friday nights, and I know Trevor, at least, often has a baseball game after school on Fridays. We don't want to lose his help. Agreed?"

Sienna looked like she'd enjoy disagreeing, but since it sounded like it was for Trevor's benefit she was stuck.

"Good. By the way, if any of you want to come to Fifth Inning tonight, you're invited. I heard our youth pastor will be giving a short inspirational thingy on prom."

Prom? Pastor John? Bailey wondered if Jenn got her wires crossed. She couldn't imagine a more unlikely topic for John to pick.

"Okay, let's get started. You know the theme, Tinseltown, right?"

Everyone nodded.

"We're going to crank it up a notch. It will be a prom like no other."

"Hey, don't we get to give ideas?" Sienna's mouth drew into an exaggerated pout. She did this a lot and seemed to think it was cute, but against Jenn's business-like manner it looked just plain whiny. "It sounds like you already have it planned, but some of us have ideas too."

"I'm sorry." Jenn stopped and looked at Sienna. "You're right, Sienna. I've gotten so excited about my own ideas that I'm getting ahead of myself. What were you thinking?"

Sienna stood up and looked around. "I don't know exactly . . . maybe we could have a room off the ballroom where we show videos—kind of like a theater."

"Oh, that would be great," a girl's sarcastic voice called out from behind Bailey. "Then all our dates could go into the theater and watch action flicks while we girls do each other's hair."

"Well, maybe it's not such a great idea, but . . ." Sienna sank back onto the bench.

"I think it would be fun," Trevor said. "I like action movies."

Sienna smiled her thanks at Trevor.

Bailey smiled too. That was one of the reasons Bailey liked Trevor. She knew from the questionnaire that Trevor liked the formal pomp of prom and that he would not want to go off and watch movies with a bunch of guys—but he also wouldn't leave a friend hanging out there with no support. Like when he sent the encouraging note to her in class.

Luke chimed in, "Let's hear what my sister has up her sleeve and maybe we can just add our ideas and work from there."

"Good idea," Jace said.

"These ideas need polishing, but let me tell you what I've been thinking." Jenn looked up toward the ceiling. "You know how retro the ballroom is at the hotel we're using—kind of art deco, golden age of Hollywood . . ."

"And?" Bailey prompted before that dreamy look could take Jenn in a whole new direction.

"And I could see taking Tinseltown to a whole new place. What if we settled on a 1930s era? You know the time in Hollywood when they had changed from the silent films to the talkies and then on to the musicals and extravaganzas?"

The group was listening but not connecting.

"Think Marlene Dietrich, Clara Bow, Douglas Fairbanks, the Marx Brothers, Charlie Chaplin, Colleen Moore . . ." Jenn looked around. "Okay, think glamorous movie stars in gorgeous gowns."

Ms. Barnard interrupted. "It sounds interesting. How do you plan to recreate this in the hotel ballroom?"

"We start with a red runner leading up to the double doors of the ballroom. The photographer will be stationed out there, looking like paparazzi. We'll get a bunch of freshman and sophomores to stand by the runway looking like adoring fans, so the photo backdrop will be our star couples against a throng of autograph-seeking fans."

"That sounds like fun," Ms. Barnard said.

Whispers of excitement had broken out throughout the group. Bailey could tell they loved it.

"The decorations inside could be simple because of the décor of the hotel. The main element will be lighting. We'll uses a flickering effect with a clicking sound, like a projector running an old black-and-white movie. It will cast a thirties theater spell over the whole room."

"It's brilliant, Jenn," Gary said.

"Thanks. I love it. Like going back in history. Reliving another era."

"Guys could even come in gangster suits, right?" The question came from one of Trevor's friends. "I mean like pinstripes. The mob was involved in early Hollywood. I read it somewhere."

"You're right," Jenn said. "And you bring up an important element. Bailey and I already talked about going vintage for prom clothes. If people haven't already bought prom clothes, they may want to dress thirties."

"But I already got a dress," Sienna said. "It's modern. Straight off the runway, like next year's style. Not off the rack."

"It's an interesting problem," Bailey said, "since many people may have already shopped. Is there some way we can blend the old and the new?"

Several kids said they didn't think it mattered what people wore, but Jenn seemed preoccupied.

"Good question," she said. "I kept worrying about the music thing. I mean I'd like to have big band music of the era, but many of you would be disappointed if we couldn't have music of our own time, right?"

A number of committee members agreed.

"If we can save money with decorations . . . I mean who wants fake palm trees anyway, right?"

Heads nodded.

"If we saved money there, could we afford a big band *and* a DJ?"

"Possibly," Ms. Barnard said.

"What if we had—let's call them—retro interludes."

"Definition, please?" Jace asked.

"I mean divide the time up between sets where the big band plays, the lights flicker and it feels like 1935. Then the lighting changes, the DJ spins his table, and it's the twenty-first century."

"It sounds like something for everyone," Ms. Barnard said. "Almost like the room is in a time warp or a flashback. I like it. What about the rest of you?"

The group loved it, and they got down to work, dividing up the tasks and setting a schedule.

"Okay, everyone, we'll meet again next Thursday. Same place, same time," Jenn said. "Don't forget, ticket people, flyers go out on Monday. Jace, you're sure you can get them designed and printed over the weekend?"

"I'm sure. I already have a design in mind—a line drawing of a Fred-and-Ginger-type couple. Because it can be black-and-white, I can work up the whole thing in Quark and run it on the machine in design lab early Monday morning." Jace's graphic design skills were the best in the school.

"Great. Prom packages have to be ready to sell the following Monday. Since we're including photography in the price, it should be easy."

"Can't they be ready earlier?" Sienna asked.

"Why?" Jenn asked.

"So many guys don't even get around to asking

anyone to prom until they have to make a decision," she said, looking at Trevor.

Uh, oh. She should have known Sienna had Trevor in her crosshairs. She figured Sienna already had a date. As a junior with no date, she must be pretty sure of herself to buy a designer dress for prom.

"I don't see how we can get it done sooner since we have to work with the photographer and hotel on the wording of the package," Jenn said. "Any other questions?" She looked around the room. "Okay. Meeting adjourned."

As the talking, laughing committee members left, Jace and Luke joined Jenn and Bailey.

"Great meeting, Jenn," Jace said draping an arm across her shoulders. "You are a natural."

Trevor joined them while his friends talked over by the double doors. "Yes, good ideas, Jenn." He turned to Luke. "Hey, do you think I can join you tonight at your Fifth Inning thing?"

Luke seemed pleased. "Sure. Want me to pick you up?"

"No, I'll drive, but I just wanted to make sure I'd know somebody there."

Jenn looked at Bailey as Trevor rejoined his friends. Her look seemed to say, "What was that about?"

7

Grab your snacks and gather around," Pastor John called.

Extra Innings had already been in full swing in the church multipurpose room for close to two hours. The evening always started with open gym. Tonight most of the kids played basketball. Others played foosball or table tennis or gathered around tables set up on the stage for visiting and watching the others play.

Trevor, Luke, and Jace all played ball. Tonight, Jenn and Bailey sat out—Jenn, because she was working on plans for prom, and Bailey, because she was afraid to put herself anywhere near Trevor. She couldn't forget the bruise on his jaw. Besides, he was still way too silent around her. She wondered if he would ever forgive her for her deception.

Ever since that baseball game, she'd given up reinventing herself. Maybe she'd be self-conscious and klutzy her whole life. If only there were a way she could change her approach to things and still be honest. She took a deep breath and shook her head. She was a total washout at this dating game. Maybe she just needed to get used to the idea of being alone for the rest of her life.

"What are you thinking?" Jenn put down her pencil and prom binder. "It looks like you are having both sides of an argument all by yourself."

"I guess I was obsessing again." Bailey gave a quick laugh. "I was wondering if I could change enough to be dateable but still be real."

"You're still thinking about Trevor's reaction to your baseball interest, huh?"

Bailey looked at Trevor, dribbling the ball down the court. "I'm not obsessed with Trevor. In fact, I'm not sure I really know him. He doesn't seem so much mad at me as distracted by something." Bailey watched him. "I know something has changed, but it's not just me; it's everything. I mean I know he was confused by my interest in baseball, and then when he thought I was with Luke . . . but that's not it."

"What is it?" Jenn asked.

"I don't know, but even his wanting to come here tonight is unusual."

Jenn smiled but didn't say anything.

"No, Jenn, it's definitely not about wanting to be around me. I can feel that, and I'm okay with that. But it's something."

"So you still want to change to try to make him take notice?"

"No, I'm letting go of that. He already noticed me." She couldn't help but laugh at that. "Now that's an understatement." The picture that came to mind was Trevor sitting there with a lapful of salsa. "If he wanted to ask me to prom, he would have done it. No, I don't want to change for Trevor—I want to change for me. I want to be more comfortable around people, to be a better friend."

"I think you're a great friend," Jenn said.

"Thanks. I guess I mean I want to be more friendly —more able to reach out to other people."

"Have you prayed about this, Bay?"

Bailey blinked her eyes. No, she hadn't.

"It might be something you just need to ask for," Jenn said.

"You're right. Why didn't that come to mind first?" Bailey wanted to shake herself. How many e-mails had she written to Ask Angela? Duh! She'd have done better to redirect those requests toward God.

"Maybe you didn't petition God because it started out being an I-want-a-date-to-the-prom thing and it seemed too silly or something."

"You're right, but look where it got me. It may have started out silly and insignificant, but it led me right into a lie that damaged a friendship. I guess nothing is too silly for prayer."

"Let's pray that God will help you overcome this

relationship block or whatever it is, and we'll see what God does, okay?"

"Okay." As Jenn went back to writing in her notebook, Bailey prayed. It looked like she was watching the game, but she asked God to forgive her for seeking answers in all the wrong places.

She continued to watch the game and offer bits and pieces of prayers until John called everyone over to the stage for his talk.

Most of the guys who had been playing basketball stretched out on the floor of the stage. A few found seats at tables.

John welcomed them and started right into his talk. "I'll bet a lot of you were surprised when you saw the topic of my talk tonight." He went to the blackboard and wrote P.R.O.M.

"Tell me you're not talking about prom tonight," said one of the basketball players.

John smiled. "That's all I've been hearing around here this spring, so I thought I'd better get in step." He turned to the board and wrote the *P* on a separate line. "Many of you know that I'm not a big fan of recreational dating. My Susan tells me that I need to stop beating you guys over the head with the courtship idea and get real with you."

Several visitors wore blank looks.

"Let me explain," John said. "My wife and I didn't believe in dating. We'd seen too many of our friends experience rejection in the process and get hurt. We liked the idea of being more prayerful and more intentional about finding the person God wanted us to marry." He stopped and took a long drink from his bottle of water.

"Boy, it's getting hard to play ball with you guys and then still have enough air to talk."

Several guys laughed.

"What I did was maintain friendships with girls but not pair off until I found Susan. I watched her for a while and got to know her until I was sure she was the type of girl I wanted to marry. Then I spoke to her father and asked him if I could court her."

Several of the kids whispered to each other. Bailey noticed Trevor cocked his head in that way he did when something interested him.

"I know," John said. "It sounds like something way too old-fashioned, but we then started to go out together and with each other's families and our love grew. It worked for us, especially since I think love is more of a decision and a commitment than it is a feeling—but I'll save that discussion for another night."

"Pastor John?" A girl across the stage raised her hand. When he nodded toward her, she asked, "Do you think it's wrong to date?"

"No. That's what Susan said I needed to address since, according to her, I'm always harping on courtship." He pulled up a chair, swung it around backwards, and sat down. "You know that sex before marriage is wrong. I don't have to tell you how that messes up people's lives and hearts, right? And you know that causing another person to weaken in his or her walk with the Lord is wrong as well. All kinds of other problems can happen in a dating relationship, but those things can happen in courtship as well, so courtship itself is no answer." He paused. "What are some other things you can see potentially wrong with dating?"

"It's not necessarily a sin," Jace said, "but dropping

all your other friends when you start going out with someone is a problem."

"Good answer," John said. "Anyone else?"

Bailey spoke up. "It's a problem when dating or the desire to date becomes overly important in your life." She should know.

John smiled. "Yes. So many things can take the top position in our lives."

Luke raised his hand. "Another danger is that a single date sometimes feels like a commitment to another person. If you go out once and never go out again, have you rejected someone? And if you feel trapped and continue to see that person because you don't know how to gracefully bow out, that's no good either." He shrugged his shoulders. "Sometimes I keep from asking someone out because I don't know if it's all right to have one fun date and not make any kind of future date."

Bailey loved that about Luke. He always thought things through and thought more about the other person's feelings than he did about his own. His sister was like that too.

"It's tough when emotions are involved, isn't it?" John said. "Anyone else want to add anything?"

"Isn't it wrong to date someone who is not a Christian?" Jenn asked quietly.

"Anyone want to take a stab at that?" John asked.

One of the basketball guys raised his hand. "Doesn't that seem kind of narrow-minded?"

A girl spoke up behind Bailey and Jenn. "Yeah. How will someone ever come to know Jesus if we avoid them?"

"All good thoughts," John said. "But let me tell you what the Bible says." John opened his Bible. "Look up

Second Corinthians." He waited while they found it in the Bibles on the tables. "Go to chapter six, verses fourteen through sixteen. Read it to yourselves." He paused. "So what does it say?"

Luke read, "Do not be bound together with unbelievers."

John nodded. "It creates a problem, doesn't it? Especially if dating is supposed to be part of the process of picking a partner for life."

He closed his Bible. "So what about Ann's idea of reaching out to the people you date with Christ's love?"

Jace spoke up. "My mom calls that missionary dating and says it's dangerous."

"Why is it dangerous?" John asked.

"You might fall in love with the person and begin coming up with all kinds of reasons why it's okay to marry them." Jace shifted in his seat. "But when you marry, if you both don't share the same faith, there's a big part of your life that's not in sync."

"That's so true," John said. "And after the newness of marriage wears off, it's often replaced with a deep sadness that you can't share the most important thing with someone you love. And when children come into the picture, it complicates it even further." He stood up again. "Sometimes it does seem narrow-minded when we focus on all these dos and don'ts, but that's the wrong focus. God gives us these guidelines because he sees the whole picture." John paused and looked around the room. "And of course he'll forgive you if you marry the wrong person or fall into one of the other traps, but he warns you because he knows that the consequences of your actions may deeply hurt you and others and jeopardize your relationship with him. Does that make sense?"

Several people nodded.

"Another quick thing. We've talked several times about being a Christian or being a believer. I didn't go into it, but if you want to know more about that, stay afterward and have a Coke with me and we'll hash that out."

He turned toward the blackboard again. "But let's get back to where we started. Let's talk about prom now."

Several of the guys groaned.

"Before you tune out, I'm not talking about dresses or big amounts of cash or limos or whatever you all do these days. Prom is an acronym for what I want to pass on to you tonight."

"An acronym?" someone said.

"First letters that form an abbreviation," Trevor said.

"Right. With all the talk of prom and all the pairing off, I started worrying that it could become more important than connecting with each other as friends, so here's what I'm asking you to do to prepare for prom."

❋   ❋   ❋

He wrote the word "pray" on the board next to the P. "We need to keep praying for each other."

"Got that." Bailey winked at Jenn.

"I'll bet you can guess what the R stands for." He paused. "Yep. Read your Bible. It's your compass. Everything you need to know can be found in its pages. Even advice about dating."

Several of the girls laughed.

"O stands for openness." He wrote that next to the O on the board. "Whether or not you are dating, you all need to be open with each other. One of the problems that happens in groups like ours when couples pair up is that people stop actively reaching out to each other."

Bailey knew that was one of the things Jenn and Jace decided to avoid when they started going out.

"And last—because it's getting late and because we are out of letters—M means to keep mixing it up. Just because you go to the prom with someone, don't let yourselves get trapped into thinking of yourselves as a couple. Until it's time to seriously look for your life partner, enjoy many relationships and treasure those friendships." He paused one more time. "So don't forget . . . P.R.O.M." He closed in prayer and the kids began to drift towards the door. As Bailey straightened chairs, she saw Trevor go up to John.

Luke waved good-bye to Trevor and found the girls. "Ready to go?" he asked. "Let's get Jace and head out."

"Do you think Trevor is talking to Pastor John about what it means to be a Christian?" Bailey asked.

"I don't know. I've been praying for him. He has seemed so preoccupied lately," Luke said.

As Bailey climbed into Luke's car, she prayed as well. *Father, whatever it is you have for Trevor . . . make it happen in his life.*

As they drove home, Luke said, "I completely forgot to tell you. I talked to Peter Lorenz, our director, at work this afternoon about Jenn's idea to borrow costumes from the archives. He said he believes they have a lending program for educational purposes, and they may be able to fit our request under that umbrella. They want you girls to come to the studio with me Monday morning. Think our parents will let us be excused from school? It's educational."

"You are kidding," Jenn said. "We'll be there."

This is just too funny, Bailey thought. *Me, the all-time Dating Dud, heading onto the set of the famous* Dating Do-Over.

Rescued from Oblivion

8

"Okay, here are the temporary security badges you need to get onto the studio property." Luke handed them plastic badges with their name printed on it under the word "visitor."

"Oh, this is too exciting," Jenn said. "Can we keep these?"

"No," Luke said, drawing out the *o*. "Think about it, little sister. If you kept the badge you could come onto the property any time you wanted or you could loan it to someone else to come onto the property. It's a security badge.

See?" He pointed to the signature of the security officer. "Security. How secure would it be if you kept it?"

"A simple *no* would be sufficient," Jenn said. "And about that 'little' as in 'little sister,' we are only minutes apart."

Bailey laughed at their sibling sparring. It was obvious that the studio was home turf to Luke.

As they walked into the building that worked as headquarters for *Dating Do-Over*, Luke introduced them to so many people they lost track of names. He knew everyone from the commissary people to the custodial staff. The building was huge—a cross between a warehouse and an office complex. When they first walked in, they came to an impressive receptionist desk with three receptionists or security people all on the phone. To the right was a floor to ceiling television made of separate panels. Each panel showed a piece of the picture. It looked funny to watch a massive face divided into four sections. Couches were arranged in this reception area and people sat around.

"They are waiting to be cleared to go backstage. That's what the security team over there on the phones are doing—checking with the guests' contact people to make sure they have appointments. I got your badges arranged in advance so we could avoid the wait."

They stepped up to the security guard at the door and showed him their badges.

"Is this your twin sister, Luke?" he asked, looking at Bailey.

"No. She's my friend. The one with the wide eyes and gaping mouth is my sister."

"Luke!" Jenn poked him in the arm.

"However do you put up with him, Miss D'Silva?" the guard said as he ushered them in through the door.

They walked past a whole row of glass conference rooms and then a number of security doors until they got to the portion of the studio used for *Dating Do-Over*. The receptionist at the desk was on the phone. "Just a minute," she mouthed to Luke.

"I don't get it," Bailey said. "This place is used for lots of shows?"

"Yes. Television shows can have a short life. They don't waste money building facilities for them. If you are creating a pilot for a new show, you find a place to set up shop and lease the place. Lots of shows share the building."

"Creating a pilot?" Jenn asked.

"Coming up with an idea for a new show. Someone gets the idea and then has to shoot a few episodes to test it out and actually create a product—create a show. Then someone else goes out to sell the show—to find a producer who'll put up the money."

"Okay, you're impressing me," Jenn said. "How did you learn so much from an after-school job?"

"To be honest, I'm not sure I've got all that straight since I just pick up the stuff from conversations and from being around it, but it's close to the way it happens." He led them over to a seating area to wait. "I'm very fortunate to have this job. Most companies just use college interns who want to get into the business. Almost nobody uses anyone younger than college."

"I wonder what's up," Luke said after a minute. "Something's wrong here." He stood up and looked around.

"People should be coming and going. See those

conference rooms over there?" He pointed to some glass rooms with conference tables and chairs. "They should have papers all over the tables and people running in and out. That's where much of the planning takes place."

He walked around the corner and came back. "This is Monday, right?"

"Yes," Jenn said. "You're making me nervous with your jumping up and down."

The receptionist signaled for them to come over.

"What's up, Kay?" Luke asked.

"Our guest fell through. It's never happened before." The receptionist seemed flustered. "She was in the hotel and all prepped and ready to go and she got word that her father died."

"How awful," Jenn said.

"We got her booked on a plane and sent her back home. They are in there now trying to figure out what to do. They'd like to just run a rerun, but they've already sold all the commercial spots." She ran her fingers through her hair. It didn't do a thing to help its already disheveled appearance.

"We'd better reschedule then and come back another time. You're not going to be needing me anyway if you're not shooting today." Luke started to turn toward the girls.

"No, wait. I'm guessing by this time they'll appreciate the interruption. I think they've been going in circles for hours." She pushed a button on her desk and the door opened behind her and she went inside.

"Wouldn't you know that when I finally get to come on set, things would be falling apart," Jenn said.

"This never happens." Luke tapped his fingers on the counter.

The door opened again and Kay said, "Go on in. Just as I guessed; they welcome the break. They asked me to get some drinks." She asked each of them what kind of soft drink they preferred before she buzzed them into the room.

Luke went in first and Jenn and Bailey followed.

"Kay told me about the upheaval today," Luke said. "I'm so sorry to hear about the guest's loss, but—"

The man at the head of the table stood up, sighed, and shook his head. "After all these years this job never gets any easier."

"Mr. Lorenz, Ms. Kimmel, Mr. Rocco, Ms. Michael, may I introduce my sister, Jenn, and her friend Bailey," Luke said as the man he called Mr. Rocco stood up as well. "Jenn and Bailey," he said, doing the second part of the introductions, "this is Mr. Peter Lorenz, director of our show."

"How do you do," both girls said together as Mr. Lorenz put out his hand, first to Jenn and then to Bailey. "Please, call me Peter." He spoke formally and talked about many years in the business, but he looked like a young Paul Newman.

"And this," Luke said extending his hand toward one of the two blonde women, "is Kiely Kimmel, though she needs no introduction. Both girls watch the show so I know they recognize you."

He went on to introduce Victor Rocco, the acting coach, and Claudia Michael, the stylist. Each one of them insisted the girls use their first names.

"I feel as if I already know you," Jenn said, "since we've spent so much time watching you."

"Please," said Peter gesturing toward seats. "Sit down."

Kay came in with a tray of soft drink cans, bottles of water, and glasses filled with ice. It took a minute for coasters, drinks, and glasses to get passed around.

"Okay, Luke told us about your theme for prom and about your idea for vintage dresses." Peter took a drink of water right from the bottle. "We loved it and wondered if we could help."

"It's so generous of you," Jenn said. "We know we could rig something up. Bailey's mom sews, but if we could borrow authentic gowns, it would make the evening unforgettable."

Claudia spoke up. "Luckily you are both slender. You have no idea how the stars of the thirties starved themselves, but I don't think you'll have any trouble fitting into the gowns."

Jenn put both of her hands on the table. "Luke said something about loaning the dresses for educational purposes. I need to be honest and say that even though the idea for the theme was mine and I'm directing the decorating, we're not official or anything. We're just girls going to a prom."

Peter laughed. "You're as honest as your brother. We knew that. Our business is built on dating so we have a soft spot for special dates. We need to sign out the gowns and need to have a reason to put next to the check-out information. Your gowns will be seen by the whole school—that's education."

"I had Kay check with our insurance agent and the gowns are covered under our policy, so you won't have to get insurance." Claudia kept looking at Bailey. "Can I ask you a personal question?"

"Sure," Bailey said, a little uncertain about where this was going.

"What color do you use on your hair to get that tone?"

Bailey laughed. "You'll have to check with God on that. It's my natural color."

"Not fair," Claudia said. "Boy, would our cameras love that color."

"So, what will your dates wear?" Kiely asked.

"My date, Jace, will rent a tuxedo. We were sort of thinking about pinstripes."

They looked at Bailey.

She took a drink. "Now there's the rub," she said, trying for humor. "I don't exactly have a date."

"Bailey was hoping to catch the eye of a guy named Trevor, but well—" Jenn stopped.

"What Jenn hates to say is that after I spilled a plate of salsa on his lap, embarrassed him in class, accidentally kicked him in the jaw, and humiliated him at his baseball game, he's not been forthcoming with an invitation."

The four at the table were laughing by the time Bailey finished.

"You know those quizzes in magazines that rate your date-ability? I never even register on their scale." Bailey figured if she couldn't laugh at her situation, she'd cry. Besides, since she'd started praying about it, she'd felt a kind of peace. She even told them about her e-mails to Ask Angela. "I may just go with Jenn and Jace if a miracle doesn't happen in the next month."

"Listen," Peter said to his team, "I've got a wild idea. Hear me out before you say no."

"I don't think we're going to say no," Kiely said. "I think we're thinking the same thing you're thinking."

"It makes sense," Victor said. "Besides, she's local, so we can start tomorrow."

"And that hair . . ." Claudia said. "I'm dying to get my hands on it."

Bailey couldn't follow the conversation, but when Claudia mentioned hair, she knew their idea involved her somehow. "I'm lost," she said.

"I'm following and I'm loving this," Jenn said. "Bailey, tell them about our attempts to reinvent you."

Luke sat there smiling.

"Jenn decided she needed to reinvent me, to make me more outgoing and more approachable. She set all kinds of tasks, like making me approach guys with a poll, having me attempt to chatter, and even trying to get me to giggle in a group. She made me over and had me keep my glasses off for a whole day."

"Sounds like it didn't work," Peter said.

"Not for lack of trying." Bailey sighed. "I'm a lost cause."

"No, you're not," Luke said.

Peter looked at Luke for a minute, then at Bailey. "I have to say I agree with Luke. You're not a lost cause."

"I'm not?" Bailey still didn't see where they were going with this. She usually wasn't this slow.

"No. You just need a *Dating Do-Over!*"

"Oh, no . . ." She felt herself backing away from the table. "The last time I tried to reinvent myself I nearly demolished an innocent guy."

"The difference is, this time, you'll do it on camera, and it will make unforgettable viewing."

Bailey could feel herself getting sucked into the vortex of a whole new quest.

The team began to mobilize. Peter took out worksheets and the team members opened their pads and started writing.

"She's a minor. Have Kay check with legal." Peter pushed the button on his intercom. "Kay, can you come in here?"

When she came in, he repeated the order and she went out to do it. He pushed the button on the intercom again. "Kay, get me Bailey's parents on the phone."

"We've lost a whole day of shooting," Kiely said. "How can we make it up?"

"And how will we line up a man for her test date? The one we had is too old for Bailey." Victor put his pencil down. "And since she's only in high school, we'll have to revise the date venues."

"Okay, hold on," Peter said. "You're bringing up a lot of potential problems, but I can see something shaping up that will frame a whole new concept here." He stood up. "Listen." He started pacing. "Listen."

"I have Bailey's mother on line two." Kay's voice over the intercom broke into Peter's pacing.

Luke and Jenn and Bailey sat quietly. The frenzy swirled around them.

Peter stopped pacing and looked at Bailey. "I didn't ask you. Are you willing to be a participant on *Dating Do-Over*?" Peter took the phone and started talking to Bailey's mom without waiting for Bailey's answer.

Bailey didn't know what to say. Just last Friday she decided to stop trying to reinvent herself and to start asking God's help instead. *God's help.* Could this be an answer to that prayer? How did she know if it was from God or not? Pastor John always said when you didn't know which way to go, seek counsel from trusted friends. "Jenn, Luke, what do you think?"

"As long as you be yourself, Bay, what harm can it do?" Jenn said.

"You know I think you're fine just the way you are," Luke said, smiling at her, "but these are my friends, and I'd love to be able to say we helped them out of a spot."

"Here Bailey." Peter handed the phone to her. "Talk to your mom."

Bailey took the phone, as Peter signaled for everyone to clear the room and give Bailey privacy. "Hi, Mom."

"My head is swimming, Bailey. Is this something you want to do?" Mom said.

Bailey could hear the M&Ms singing in the background. Everything seemed so normal at home. "I think so, Mom, but I need your input. On Friday I stopped trying to manage things myself and I asked God to take over in my situation. I was tired of trying to organize things so I could get a date."

"And you're wondering if this is God's way of helping you?"

"Well, it seems like such a miracle. I mean it's not like it's solving world hunger or anything, but . . ."

"That's the wonderful thing about the Lord, honey. He cares deeply about world hunger, but he also cares deeply about you. If having a prom date's important to you, it's important to God."

"What do you think, Mom?"

"I think it will be fun. As long as you keep your head and keep the Lord topmost. Having a makeover and learning new people skills will only be a plus. I'll call your father and make sure it's okay with him. I'll call the school as well. I wish I could take off to be with you, but we're short of subs during the end of flu season and finding sitters for the girls—well you know. Do you think they could arrange to have Jenn stay with you over these four days?"

"I'll ask."

"This is exciting, honey. If you don't hear from me in the next couple of minutes, consider it a go. I'll see you when you get home."

As soon as she hung up the phone, they filed back in along with Luke and Jenn. She smiled. They must have all been circled around the phone out there, waiting to see the line-in-use light go out.

"I think it's okay. My mother's calling my dad to check. Then she's calling our school."

"Good," Peter said.

"She wanted to know if there's any way for Jenn to stay with me." Bailey felt funny asking. "My mom teaches school and could never get off on such short—"

"No problem if Jenn can make arrangements with her parents and with school."

One by one, the team dispatched every single problem. Bailey could hardly wait to hear Peter's ideas, until she remembered the horror of a plate of salsa landing on Trevor's lap despite her best intentions. She could only imagine how that would have played on national TV.

What have I gotten myself into?

Dating Disaster

9

O**kay**, listen up. We've lost all our planning time. There's no time for
evaluation, for all of our tests, for personality
analysis. We're going to see how good we really
are. This one's going to be by the seat of our
pants."

"I think we're up for the challenge," Kiely
said.

Bailey wondered how big a challenge it
would be.

"Because we lost a whole day plus several
weeks of planning, we need to make the test

date happen tonight." He looked at Luke. "Can you fill in as my assistant on this episode? I think I'm going to need your input and your help."

"Sure. I'd love to." Luke seemed eager.

"Okay, picture this. We promote the show to teen markets—sell it on the prom angle. Bailey is sweet—what—seventeen?"

Bailey nodded.

"Okay, sweet seventeen and never been out. Prom is looming and she has no date. We step in to get her 'prom ready.'"

"But prom is not for three and a half weeks," Luke said.

"No problem," Peter said. "We'll want the prom sequence to replace the dream date sequence—this show will be all new. A new twist. We'll promote it big. I wonder if we can work it into sweeps . . ."

When he went off on these rabbit trails, he began thinking out loud. Bailey could see team members writing as fast as he talked, getting down all his ideas.

"Exciting stuff," Kiely said, "but back to the schedule. We usually shoot in one tight week and give ourselves a few weeks to edit and run the segment within about a month." She turned to the girls. "We do not have the luxury of time since we do this on a weekly basis. There are no episodes banked for the future. That's why we hit our crisis this morning."

"Here's what we do," Peter said. "We shoot in four days, and we edit the whole thing and have it ready to go. We wait three weeks and shoot the final scene at the prom. That can be dropped in inside of a day. Then it pops right into the schedule."

"Next problem," Victor said. "How do we arrange a demonstration date for tonight?"

"What time is it? Eleven a.m.?" Peter drummed fingers on the table. "We don't have any college freshman on the date list do we?"

Kiely shook her head.

Bailey's stomach began to tighten. She could barely talk to guys she went to school with every day. What in the world would she do with someone she'd never met on a date? She knew these test dates were supposed to go awry, but did they have any idea what they were in for?

"Wait a minute," Peter jumped out of his chair. He rubbed his hands together as he paced behind the chairs.

He reminded Bailey of one of her friends when she was in elementary school who was always referred to as hyperactive. She smiled. Maybe hyperactive was just a matter of too many big ideas to fit in one confined space.

"Okay, listen . . ."

Bailey already figured out that he prefaced each new idea with the word *listen.* She looked around the room. The team sat with pencils poised, ready to take down his words. How exciting it was to be in on the planning of an episode like this.

"Instead of a demonstration date, what do you say we make arrangements to go over to school and film reenactments of three of Bailey's worst incidents with— was it Trevor?"

Bailey's stomach clenched into a knot. "No—"

"It's not Trevor? What is his name?"

"No. I mean, yes, his name is Trevor, but no, you can't make me go through that again."

Peter sat down in the empty chair beside her. "The reason we do the test date is because we have to have some frame of reference. How can the good be good if we don't see how bad the bad is?"

"Besides," Victor said, "you have no idea how much fun this will be for our audience. With your gorgeous red hair and the way you described these incidents, I bet these will have an *I Love Lucy* feel to them."

Jenn laughed, adding, "Now that you mention it, they sort of had that feel in real life."

"Thanks a lot, Jenn." The whole idea of a dating makeover sounded like fun until they came up with this idea of involving the whole school. *God, can this be of you?* She thought about Pastor John's *O* in his talk on P.R.O.M. *Openness. He said we needed to stay open with each other.* This was laying her problem wide open to the whole student body. Of course, even if she didn't involve the school at this point, once the episode aired, her life would be an open book anyway.

"Did we lose you, Bailey?" Peter asked.

"No, I was just considering all the angles. I hate to bare all my klutziness before the whole world, but I guess that sometimes, until you put all your problems out there, you won't be able to find a solution."

"So you're okay with this?" Peter asked.

When she nodded, he said, "Victor and Claudia, take these three to lunch and do your own evaluations in each of your areas. When you're done, bring them to the school for filming."

Kay had come into the room in answer to some kind of silent summons. "Kay, I need you to get releases ready—dozens of them. Go out to the school where Bailey's mom works and get her to sign one first, then meet me at San Vincente High. You're going to be calling parents and arranging releases. If we can get a school official as a witness, I think we can do these over the phone. We'll pay scale for extras, so I think we need W-4s as well."

Bailey felt as if a steamroller had been fired up.

"I'll head out to the school and get the principal in our corner, and then we'll make this happen. Let's plan on four o'clock in the cafeteria."

❋　　　❋　　　❋

As they pulled into the parking lot, Luke had to drive around to find a space to park his car. Victor and Claudia were also looking for a place to park Victor's Maserati.

"Do you think we should tell Victor that a high school parking lot is not exactly the safest place for a Maserati?" Luke said with a laugh.

"I don't think fingerprints and drool stains are fatal," Jenn said.

"Everyone's cars are still here. It is four in the afternoon on a Monday, isn't it?" Bailey asked.

Luke laughed. "Looks like Peter's been here. Can you believe the guy? It's like this all the time. I'll bet he charmed everyone here at school." He finally found a place about as far as he could have gotten from the cafeteria. "He's probably already shot footage of the school and managed to gather the trustees together for a brief cameo with the principal. By now, they've moved heaven and earth to make it all happen for him."

"I can't believe his energy," Jenn said.

"But how is he going to get Trevor to take part in the reenactments? It was painful the first time."

"They won't really have you kick him again," Luke said. "Makeup will do the bruise."

Bailey just closed her eyes.

Luke turned around and looked into the backseat. "Bailey, Trevor will do this because he considers you a friend and will want to help you out."

"I think he'd like to forget I ever existed," Bailey said.

"I don't think so. Something's going on with Trevor. He doesn't open up easily, but I don't think it's you." Luke sighed. "I'm still praying for him. I'm not sure he has any friends he really talks to."

"You might be right, Luke," Jenn said. "He mostly seems to have hangers-on."

"Anyway, unless we get out of the car, we'll never get this over with." Luke got out and went around and opened the door for Jenn and Bailey.

"There's Victor and Claudia looking lost," Jenn said.

When the two team members spotted Luke, Jenn, and Bailey, they all walked into the cafeteria together.

"Good. You're here," Peter said. "Everything's a go. Mr. Harder has been wonderful. By the way, Victor, I promised him you would come on a day when we're on hiatus to speak to the drama club about method acting."

Victor took out his leather planner and made a note.

"And, Claudia, we are auctioning off a complete Claudia Michael makeover at the next PTA auction."

Claudia also made a note. She had a big smile on her face. Apparently, Peter Lorenz was a world-class negotiator. The school would gain national attention, plus a couple of major perks. Knowing Mr. Harder, he'd have the journalism class prepare press releases about Victor's acting class and the Claudia Michael makeover auction to get all the more attention from the press. Good media coverage only enhanced the school's reputation, and whenever the next bond measure came up . . .

Bailey had to smile.

"I think we're ready. The cafeteria staff recreated the meal—salsa and all—and we have more than enough on-camera extras."

"Did Trevor agree to do this?" Bailey asked.

"Yes. He wanted to help you out. We got parent releases and we're good to go."

Bailey felt relieved. Maybe Luke was right. Maybe Trevor *was* a friend.

"Of course, the money was a big issue with Trevor. I've never had someone negotiate so hard. We've ended up paying him more than Victor gets per episode."

"Oh." Bailey's shoulders dropped. *Money. So much for friendship.*

"Here's how it's going to play out. The film crew already filmed background stuff all over the school for us to use in the editing process. Done." Peter always sounded like he had a checklist in his brain.

"We're going to film the salsa sequence, then you'll both run and change for the kick-in-the-teeth segment."

"It wasn't in the teeth," Bailey said. "It was right on the jaw."

"We're just calling it that in our notes."

Bailey was beginning to feel a little cranky. "So who did you get to do the sabotage to my backpack that caused the whole thing?"

Ms. Barnard, who was standing nearby, got that look

on her face. Bailey remembered that she had wanted the culprit, if found, to receive discipline. Oops.

"A girl named . . . let's see, Sienna, volunteered. She didn't say anything about sabotage, but she said she was the one whose arm accidentally caught the strap on your backpack and toppled you. She wanted to make sure she got into the filming."

I'll bet she did.

Ms. Barnard nodded her head slightly. Bailey could tell the outcome would not be good for Sienna.

"After we finish that part, we'll change again before we go out to the baseball field."

"Not the baseball field!" Bailey couldn't help herself. This one, the deception, hurt the most. The other two were accidents.

"The baseball incident is important," Peter said. "That's the one we're going to use to show that change can be genuine. Even though we have our acting coach, it's not about being something we're not. It's about being better as ourselves."

Bailey put her hands in the air. "I give up."

"Good. Trust us. We don't do anything to embarrass." He turned to the crowd to make an announcement. "Okay, people. Time is unbelievably tight. We only have about three and a half hours of daylight so there can be no mistakes. Extras, if you hold us up in any way, you're off the shoot."

Bailey looked around at the crowd. They didn't make a sound. Amazing. Peter Lorenz should be a high school teacher.

"Okay, everything's set up like it was. Here's your clipboard, Bailey. Where's Trevor?"

Someone went and got Trevor. Without looking at

Bailey, he sat down where he sat that awful day. Bailey sat down next to him.

"Are you two ready?"

They both nodded.

"Roll film."

Bailey went through the questionnaire with him again. His answers were still interesting to her, so she knew she probably didn't look like she was playacting. In fact, she felt Trevor relaxing as well. It confused Bailey. It felt like they could be friends.

Just then his group of friends came up behind him and began their heckling. Sienna was the loudest again. It felt exactly the same as it did the other day. Bailey could feel her shoulders getting tight.

She jumped up and told Trevor she'd catch him later for the rest of the questions and, like clockwork, the metal part of the clipboard caught the edge of the tray and flipped it onto them. It didn't take any special effects to recreate the mess.

Trevor jumped up with a shocked look on his face and she started to grab napkins to dab at him.

Just then his friends began their taunts about an April Fool's Day joke. The look on Trevor's face changed from one of shock to one of deep hurt.

Either he was the best actor in the world or he was, like Bailey, reliving this all over again.

"And . . . cut," Peter called. "Perfect in one try. Amazing. Get out of those clothes and let's meet right here in ten minutes."

The janitors moved in to clean up the mess as Jenn and Claudia took Bailey toward the bathroom.

"You poor thing," Claudia said. "Did it really happen that way?"

"Sadly enough, that was practically exact."

"Every one of our viewers will be cringing, but then they'll be pulling for you for the rest of the show."

Once they assembled in the cafeteria, Peter called everyone to take their places again. Bailey sat down next to Trevor.

"Remember, Bailey," Trevor whispered, "they plan to do the bruise with makeup."

Bailey saw the smile on his face and laughed. Maybe it wasn't all about money. Maybe he was a friend. The money thing didn't seem like Trevor at all.

"I just hope we can reenact this. I have no idea how it happened. It seems like such a freak thing. How can you make it happen again?"

Peter overheard. "You're right. In order for this to happen, everything needs to be exact—almost like a science experiment. You two need to make sure you're sitting at the same angle and about the same distance apart." He turned toward Sienna. "You need to catch the backpack exactly the same way for this to happen. This was where you'd taken your glasses off for vanity, right Bailey?"

"Thanks for sharing that with the world, Peter." Bailey grimaced, but at this point, it hardly mattered. Her life would be an open book.

"It's just that if everything is the same, it should happen again. It's physics."

He looked around the room. "Extras in place? Quiet everyone." He paused. "Roll film."

It felt like Bailey had gone two weeks back in time. She sat in the same place, said the same things, and still squinted to see Trevor. *Oh, that will look attractive on camera.*

Out of the corner of her eye she saw a blur. Sienna. It had been Sienna that day. She recognized the movement. The blur bumped into her backpack and jostled her forward a little.

"Cut." Peter went to the camera and looked in the window. He must have been looking at the scene. "Sienna, you can't have just bumped the backpack—that sent Bailey forward. It had to have been a backward pull."

Sienna looked uncomfortable. "Maybe the backpack caught on something."

Ms. Barnard moved closer in and motioned to Mr. Harder to join her. She whispered something to him.

"Are you carrying the same stuff as you did that day?"

"Yes?" Sienna made it sound like a question.

Peter went over to inspect her.

Luke leaned in to Bailey and Trevor. "She's tangled with the wrong guy here. He used to produce real-crime documentaries."

"Sienna," Peter said impatiently, "there's not a single thing that could catch on something."

Bailey heard Jenn whisper, "The girl needs to call her lawyer."

"Could it be your arm caught the strap of the backpack?"

"You mean accidentally?" Sienna asked.

"Whatever."

"Maybe."

"Then can we please try it the way it happened?" Peter looked at his watch. "Roll film."

They did it again, but this time the blur jerked the backpack backward slightly. It only rotated Bailey around so her knees bumped Trevor's.

"Cut." Peter turned to Sienna. "You're off the shoot." Then he turned toward the extras. "Someone in drama . . . you've seen Sienna do the movement twice. I need someone her height and weight to take her place. I'll tell you what to do."

Mr. Harder stepped forward. "Carrie, can you do it?"

The girl nodded and came over to Peter.

"Thanks, Carrie. We'll raise you from extra pay to scale. Kay will take care of you afterward. Here's what I want you to do. Walk by Bailey just like Sienna did, but when you get behind her, grab the right shoulder strap of her backpack and jerk down, fast and hard."

Peter ran her through the actions without the final jerk.

Bailey heard Ms. Barnard say, "Sienna, don't leave. Mr. Harder wants to see you after the filming is over."

They went through the sequence of events again with Bailey starting to get up to leave. She saw the blur and felt the same sharp tug on her backpack. Her foot flew up and came within an inch of breaking Trevor's nose. Trevor reached out and grabbed her before her head could hit the floor.

"And cut."

"That was a little too close," Trevor said. "The flinch you'll see on film was not fake."

"It sure looked real enough," Peter said. "We lost some time there but that's a wrap. Let's change again and do the baseball scene. The team has been out there all this time. It's probably the longest warm-up they've ever had."

After they changed clothes, Trevor sat down in his baseball uniform with Claudia and got his makeup bruise. It looked as real as the first one. As Jenn, Luke, and Bailey walked out to the baseball field, Trevor caught up with them. When they got to the field, Luke and Jenn started up the bleachers but Trevor stopped Bailey. "I'm so sorry about that last incident," he said. "I had no idea about Sienna."

Bailey didn't say anything.

"I've been distracted," he said, almost under his breath. "I've got some personal problems."

"It wasn't your fault, Trevor. No apology necessary." Bailey let out a breath. "I'm just glad it wasn't my fault either."

They stood silently watching the warm-up for a couple of minutes. "Do you want to talk about what's going on, Trevor?" Bailey asked.

"No." He swallowed hard. "I can't."

Picking Up the Pieces

10

The baseball segment went well, but it had to be filmed twice. This time it was the camera crew's fault. When Bailey stood up and yelled "offsides," they laughed so hard they bumped the camera.

As the crew packed up, Peter came over to Bailey. "It can't have been easy for you to relive these scenes, but you have no idea how funny they are."

"Actually, they are a little more amusing the second time around," Bailey admitted.

"Go home and get some sleep. First thing

tomorrow, we'll film what we call 'the debrief.' We'll talk separately to you and to Trevor and get your take on the date . . . or in your case, the encounters. You will watch some film clips of the scenes and our experts will evaluate your actions on camera with you."

"Oh fun." Bailey laughed. "This whole thing only gets better, doesn't it?"

Peter laughed. "I'll tell you this—the reason this episode is going to be so strong is because of your wonderful ability to laugh at yourself. You'll see."

❁   ✳   ❁

Jenn and Luke came early in the morning to pick up Bailey for the ride to the studio.

"Do we have time to eat breakfast?" Bailey asked. "Mom made omelets."

"Sure. It'll be a whole lot better than the stale donuts laying around the studio," Luke said.

"Hi, Debbie. Hi, Jim," Jenn said as she walked into the kitchen. She had long since taken Bailey's parents up on their request that she use their first names.

"Hi, Mr. and Mrs. Tollefson," Luke said. "Thanks for the invite to breakfast."

"Yeah. Our mom never has time to do a hot breakfast on school mornings," Jenn said.

Mom laughed. "Neither do I. Counting today, this is two times in about as many years. It's just that it seems like a special day."

"I'll say it's special." Luke paused with his fork halfway to his mouth. "The school made arrangements for all three of us to be off this whole week without

126

having to make up work. They'll count our television adventure as work experience."

"Well, for you, it is work experience, right?" Dad asked.

"I know. It's a wonderful chance to be able to see what it's like to be an assistant to the director."

The three sat down. Dad prayed and Mom dished up plates. Mallory and Madeline ate quietly. It must have been the novelty of guests at breakfast.

"Mmm," Jenn said, "this omelet is delicious—jack cheese and avocado?"

Mom nodded. "So today they film?" She paused. "You seem a little . . . dressed down, Bailey."

"Yep. I'm supposed to be my old geeky self. You know, the 'before' part." Bailey sketched the quote marks in the air.

"Oh. Gotcha." Mom took a bite. "The only thing I'm a little worried about—"

"A little worried?" Dad laughed. "That's an understatement. She worried into the wee hours."

"Okay," Mom said with a grin, "I'm worried about your date for the prom. Usually on the show, contestants go out and meet dates on the street and learn how to introduce themselves. Later they pick the best one and ask that person out."

"Don't worry, Mom. I'm not going to pick up some guy off the street for my prom date." She made a funny face. "I wish you had told me you were wasting time worrying about this. I could have saved you the wasted sleep time. Peter is doing the show totally different. He's making it kind of a junior version of the regular show."

"I think he's actually considering it a pilot for a possible spin-off," Luke said, forking the last bite in his mouth. "He hasn't said as much, but I haven't seen him this excited in a long time."

"When they've finished my *Dating Do-Over* training and the makeover, I'll have to pick someone from the guys at school to ask for a date to the prom."

Dad got that concerned look going with his eyebrows.

"I know it's not traditional for me to do the asking, Dad, but this is kind of like a sporting event or a challenge. I'm going to play the game the best I can."

"I'm just glad they are making it age-appropriate," Mom said.

"Hey guys, we've got to go." Jenn stood up and took her plate to the sink. "Thanks so much for breakfast, Debbie." She gave Mallory and Madeline each a hug.

"See you tonight," Bailey said to her family.

❋　　　❋　　　❋

When they got to the studio, the team—minus Kiely—was still huddled in the conference room.

"Where's Kiely?" Luke asked.

"She and the film crew are over at San Vincente High debriefing with Trevor. They should be back soon."

"You mean I don't get to hear what he said?" Bailey asked.

"Not while he's being interviewed. It would make it too difficult to get an honest assessment if you were standing there listening." Peter made a note on his clipboard. "But we'll show it to you after we do your debrief."

"Okay, here's the schedule," Peter said, handing

them a sheet of paper. "First comes the segment where you watch the footage from the test date and do your debrief interview. Then you can watch the raw footage of Trevor's debrief. That will take up today."

"That almost gets us back on schedule, doesn't it?" Luke asked.

"It sure does," Peter said. "Yesterday morning if you'd told me we'd be here today, I'd never have believed it. It's almost like God dropped this in our laps."

Bailey smiled.

Peter looked at his schedule again. "In the morning, Victor will teach you how to own a room."

"Own a room?" Jenn asked. "How can she own a room?"

"You'll see what I mean tomorrow," Victor said. "It's a technique from method acting."

"In the afternoon, Bailey, you'll be bussing tables at Upstart Crow with Kiely."

"Okay, I'm not even going to ask." Bailey shifted from one foot to the other.

"Thursday, we'll all head back to school for you to choose the guy you'd like to ask to the prom. The cameras will roll as you do the asking."

"I don't even want to think about that now." Bailey's mouth had gone dry.

"Don't panic. By then you'll have excellent training under your belt and it will be easy. You'll know exactly what to do."

"Yeah, right," Bailey said, under her breath.

"You'll have lunch and then head to Rodeo Drive for some shopping."

Jenn's eyes got round. "And I'll get to go as well?"

"And I *won't* have to go?" Luke added.

"Yes and yes," Peter said, laughing. "In fact, we plan to offer a good segment on prom dresses, so we may use you as well, Jenn. You can help model. The companies that make prom dresses are over the moon about this episode, and we're already talking about rerunning it multiple times next year during prom-dress buying season."

"Rabbit trail, Peter," Claudia cautioned. "He just can't keep the glee out of his voice when it comes to promotional fees."

Victor put on his best announcer voice and intoned, "Promotional fees have been paid for by the makers of prom dresses the world over."

Peter ignored their ribbing. "Of course, after trying on dozens of dresses, you'll end up coming back to the studio archives and doing vintage."

"I can't wait." This was the part both Bailey and Jenn looked forward to.

"Friday, Claudia will take you to the salon and do the hair and makeup segments. We'll make it look like we're doing it on the actual day of prom." Peter made a note. "We will, of course, do hair and makeup again on the day of the prom, but we want all the filming finished except for the actual prom footage." Peter looked up at them over his glasses. "Sorry. Can you tell I'm in midshow mania? Please, sit down. Do you have any questions?"

No one asked any, so he went on. "Luke, can I get you to check the set we're using for the debrief and make sure it's ready? Claudia, take the girls to the green room."

"Yes sir," she said and saluted.

Peter smiled. "A bit autocratic, eh?"

"No worse than usual."

"Tell, me, Claudia," Jenn asked, looking around at the huge room, "what is a green room?"

"It's the room where people wait and relax before going on air. That's why it's so comfortable—to soothe jitters."

"It's not working." Bailey walked around the room, running her hand over the counter of the snack area and poking into the drawers in the hair and makeup room. She had enough jitters for all of them.

Jenn came over and looked at the makeup palettes with Bailey. "A little nervous?"

"Nervous is when I have to walk into a new homeroom class and say 'hi' to people. This is terrified."

A man came into the room with some small black boxes and wires.

"Bailey," Claudia said, "this is Brent—our sound tech. He's going to mic you and run a sound check."

He handed one of the black boxes to Bailey. "Clip this to the back of your jeans. Then take this mic and run the cord up the front of your top and clip the mic right there on the collar near your throat."

Bailey turned away from him and ran the wire like he said, clipping the mic on the collar. "Okay?"

"There's a little on/off switch here on the top of the box. You need to practice switching it on and off until you get to know which is which. You'll be wearing this thing a lot this week and embarrassing things can happen if you leave it on by mistake."

"Okay, I don't want to even think about that." Bailey reached behind her and did the on/off thing.

"Now speak in a natural voice and let me get a volume for you."

"One, two, three . . ."

Kiely came in. "Hi, Bailey. Hey, Claude. Hi, Jenn. Let me run a comb through my hair, put on fresh lipstick, and we'll be good to go."

"I'll go check to make sure the dating disaster film is ready," Claudia said.

"And I always thought you were just the stylist," Jenn said.

"There's no way we could do a show like this without rolling up our sleeves and getting into every part of it. But we love it. There's never a dull moment." Claudia gave a little wave as she walked out the door.

"Okay, ready?" Kiely looked at Bailey. "There's no need to get nervous. We're going to have fun here. Luckily this is not live, so we can do it as many times as needed. Of course, your first reaction is usually the best, so if we can get it in one, we'll be thrilled. Victor will be with me to analyze your actions, okay?"

Bailey meant to say "okay," but nothing came out.

"Let's get you settled in." Kiely turned to Jenn. "Do you want to wait here where it's comfortable, or do you want to come onto the sound stage with us?"

Bailey shot her a pleading look.

"I'll come."

They walked out of the green room and past a guard at a set of double doors. The doors were covered with different versions of "keep out" and "unauthorized."

"Okay, here's our set." Kiely opened the door to what looked like a warehouse with a raised platform that had walls and a rug, plus lots of plants and pillows and comfy looking furniture in it.

"Cool." Jenn walked around it. "I always thought you were meeting in a loft somewhere. It looks just like a living room."

"Yeah," Bailey said, "except when you're in it and you look out and see all those cameras and wires and the fact it's on a stage and—"

Jenn made a tsk-tsk sound. "You need to lighten up and just try to enjoy this experience. It's only once in a lifetime, Bay."

"I know, but I'm so nervous."

Jenn lowered her voice and put a hand of Bailey's arm. "Lord, calm Bailey. Remind her that even though this is Hollywood, you are right there on that stage with her. Let her have fun this week."

"Amen," Bailey said.

Kiely and Victor were already seated in their chairs flanking her empty one. "You ready?"

"I am now," Bailey said, whispering a thank-you to Jenn.

"Okay, get comfortable." Kiely paused. "Ready?"

Bailey nodded.

"I'm Kiely Kimmel and this is our acting coach, Victor Rocco, and we're here with our special guest, Bailey Tollefson."

Peter and Luke came in the door soundlessly and gently closed it behind them. Bailey felt less alone with Jenn and Luke in the room.

"As we told you at the outset, this show is very different because instead of being a young urban single, Bailey is a high school senior." Kiely turned her smile on Bailey. "Bailey, when it comes to dating, how would you describe yourself?"

Bailey tried to look like she was considering that

question. "That's hard to say, Kiely, since I've never once been out on a real date."

"Hmmm. Sweet seventeen and never been . . ." Kiely laughed at the unspoken phrase. "I understand that you're pretty shy around guys."

Bailey relaxed a little. Maybe she could handle this after all. Kiely would ask her questions, and she would answer as honestly as she could. "If I were just shy that would be okay, but I tend to try too hard, and then I get klutzy. So I either sit there like a rock, or I trip and fall at the guy's feet."

Victor laughed.

"A few weeks ago, I decided I had to overcome this if I stood any chance of getting a date for my senior prom."

"So what did you do?" Kiely asked.

"My friend had me collect data for a poll. It was directed toward guys so I could get comfortable talking with them."

"And we were able to film three of those encounters . . . as it happened, all with the same guy, Trevor. Let's watch them and see how you did."

They ran the first sequence. It was painful for Bailey to watch. She actually did well on the questionnaire part, but when the salsa part came she lowered her head and buried it in her hands.

"I guess we could call that a memorable impression." Kiely smiled. Victor couldn't stop laughing on Bailey's other side. He hadn't been there to see the filming, and apparently he found this hilarious.

"But you got another chance with this young man, didn't you?" Kiely asked.

"Yes. He agreed to finish my questionnaire despite the salsa disaster."

"Let's watch and see how that went." Kiely leaned in toward the monitor. "Same place, different time, right?"

"Right," Bailey said. As she watched, she was pleasantly surprised. She seemed at ease with Trevor until his friends came. Then she watched the scene with Carrie as Sienna. The meanness of it practically took her breath away.

When the film stopped, Kiely said, "It doesn't look like that was your fault. It didn't turn out well, but Victor, what would you say about Bailey's approach to Trevor?"

Victor leaned in toward the camera, elbows on his knees. "As you sat down and began to listen to his answers, your whole body posture changed. You visibly relaxed and seemed to be enjoying yourself. It wasn't until the accident that this one went bad. I'd say you're too hard on yourself."

"Okay," Kiely said, smiling into the camera. "Now for the last one."

"Wait." Bailey help up her hand, palm toward the camera. "Before we see that, can I come clean?"

Kiely laughed. "Go ahead."

"I was still working on being charming enough to attract a certain guy's attention. In the Ask Angela column in *Metro Girl Magazine,* she said it's important to be interested in the things your guy is interested in." Bailey swallowed and licked her lips. "When Trevor mentioned baseball, I lied and told him I loved baseball."

Kiely grimaced and said, "Uh, oh."

"I set about it seriously. I studied sports books for

two full days. Unfortunately, I included all sports. All the terms sort of ran together in my mind."

"Let's watch," Kiely said. They ran the footage of the baseball game and even the sound technician was shaking in silent hysterics.

"So what went wrong?"

"I lied and got caught in my lie. It was embarrassing, and I had to ask Trevor's forgiveness."

"You did?" Victor said, caught by surprise.

"Anyway," Bailey said, "you can see what a complete dork I am around boys. If *Dating Do-Over* can help, I'll be forever grateful."

Peter raised his arms. "And . . . two . . . three . . . cut. Great debrief."

"The film clips are wonderful. Have we ever had stuff quite so dramatic and funny before?" Kiely asked.

"I don't know. It's pretty funny stuff." Peter turned toward the crew. "Okay, it's good. Let's break for lunch, and then we'll look at Trevor's debrief and call it a day."

❋   ❋   ❋

Late that afternoon, as they rode home in Luke's car, none of them said too much.

Bailey couldn't stop thinking about Trevor's interview. He insisted that he didn't see Bailey as socially inept. He said he liked her. At another point, he said he considered her a friend—one of the few he had these days.

It made Bailey sad. If he considered her a friend, what kind of friend was she? She didn't even know what kind of problem weighed on his mind.

11

Good morning, Bailey." Victor gave a sweeping gesture of welcome as Bailey walked in the door. This set looked almost like a ballet studio, complete with mirrors against the wall and a barre attached to the mirrors. The wood floor shone under the lights and looked as if dancers had practiced there for hundreds of years. A perfect, artful setting if it weren't for the fact that it was just a studio set with only two walls in the same huge warehouse-like building.

Ever since the baseball game, Bailey had

committed herself to being real. Would she be able to do that on a sound stage with an acting coach? The good thing was that she liked Victor. *We'll give it a try.*

"Hi, Victor. Are you ready for me?"

"I guess the question is, are *you* ready for *me*?"

"The funny thing is, I was just pondering that very question."

He laughed. "We're going to let the crew start filming right away so they can get plenty of footage to use. This segment will actually only be four minutes long when edited, but I want them to have plenty to work with. So don't be nervous. Hardly anything you say will end up on the show."

"Okay." Bailey saw Jenn and Luke settle in over against a wall in the darkness. She could barely see them. It was a shame. Jenn always made her feel more at ease. And Luke . . . ? Well, she didn't know how she felt about Luke. The more time she spent with him, the more she liked him. She loved his quiet faith for one thing, and he never seemed to judge others. Like at the baseball game—he never seemed to think less of her for acting like a fool. Plus seeing him around his work impressed her. *Integrity.* That was the word for what Luke had. Everyone trusted him. Jenn was so lucky to have him as her brother.

"Are you tired?" Victor asked. "You seem a little distracted."

"Sorry. I'm just thinking, but I'll focus now. Let's go."

"Guys, you want to start rolling film? Bailey, can you go out that door in the set and come back in, much like you came in the first time this morning?"

"Okay." Bailey went out through the door. It seemed solid enough even though it was set in a fake wall.

When she came back through, she closed it carefully to make sure not to knock down the whole set. Well aware of the cameras, she came in a few feet and stopped and looked around at the set again. Nothing had changed . . . mirrors and barre and beautiful floor.

"Good morning, Bailey," Victor said in that self-confident voice of his. He came over to her with his hand outstretched.

She backed up a little but put out her hand. She knew she should try to be bright, but it felt funny to be so chirpy with a hello. "Hi, Victor."

He pulled up a chair, swung it around backward, and mounted it, almost like a horse. "Please, get a chair and sit down."

Bailey went over and found a straight-back chair like his and placed it a short distance from his and sat down, crossing her legs at the ankle and intertwining her fingers.

"When I looked at your dating disaster footage, I noticed you always look a little demure," he said.

"Explain *demure*. I think I know what you mean, but I'm not sure."

He stood up, turned his chair around, sat down with his knees together, crossed his ankles, and intertwined his fingers.

Bailey burst out laughing. "Oh, you mean ladylike."

He opened his legs and relaxed again. "It's more than ladylike or just being reserved. It's like you curl in on yourself. You try to make yourself as small as you can. You almost seem to protect your middle."

"I do?"

He nodded. "When you walked into this room, you barely stepped in the door. You took a few steps, but then you looked around and assessed the room. I'll bet you could tell me every escape."

Bailey laughed. He had her there. In a normal room she could always do that.

"If people asked you what kind of personality you have, what would you say?"

"I guess I'd say I'm shy or socially inept."

"My job today is to give you skills to overcome those traits. Do you know what shyness is about?"

"Is it low self-esteem?"

"Maybe partly, but shyness is really just being overly aware of yourself. If you can take the focus off yourself and how uncomfortable you feel and put it on other people, you'll find yourself able to overcome shyness."

That sounded too easy. "Are you sure?"

"Repeat this sentence, 'It's not about me.'"

"It's not about me," Bailey said obediently.

"You need to learn to repeat that to yourself whenever you are feeling uncomfortable. We saw you doing those questionnaires with guys at school. You looked totally comfortable. Why did that work so well?"

Bailey knew how to answer from years of having to answer teachers' leading questions. "It was not about me?"

"Exactly!" Victor seemed pleased. "I want to teach you to own the room as soon as you walk into it."

"Own the room?"

"You came into this room as if you didn't really have a right to be here. People love confidence, and you need to come into the room with confidence. Do you have any idea how you will do that?"

Another leading question. Bailey thought for a moment. "By realizing it's not about me and looking for other people to focus on."

"Bingo!" Victor smiled. "That's the secret to feeling comfortable in any social situation. You just take charge and try to make others feel at ease. At first you'll be acting; but like with any skill you learn, it will become part of you."

"But I don't want to act. You saw my footage of the baseball game when I was pretending to be something I'm not. I decided then I wanted to be real."

"Here's the difference, Bailey. I want to teach you a life skill. When you were a little baby, you were a crawler, and that was real. But the time came for you to learn to walk. As you practiced, you became a walker. Good thing, too, since it would be hard to get around Los Angeles as an adult who still had to crawl." Victor smiled. "Am I making any sense? What I'm trying to say is that it's a good thing to avoid deception, but learning and applying new skills is growing, not pretending."

"You've sold me, Victor." Bailey liked what he had to say. Maybe trying to reinvent herself was not all wrong. "I do want to grow, and I like the idea of focusing on other people; so show me how I do this."

"Okay, watch me." Victor went out the set door and came back in. He walked in confidently as if looking for someone. He came right over to her. "Hello, Bailey. It's good to see you." He stopped, dropped his confident stance, and turned toward her. "What did I do there?"

"You came into the room and focused on me immediately."

"Right, I came in like I owned the room, didn't I?" He pointed toward the door. "Now you try."

Bailey went out the door. This time when she came in, she wouldn't worry about being careful. *After all, I own this room.* She laughed. As she stepped in the door, she focused immediately on Victor. *It's not about me.* "Victor," she said, putting out her hand. "How are you?" She crossed the distance toward Victor and grasped his hand in a warm handshake. "Here, let me get you a chair." She went over, got a chair, and put it down for Victor.

"You've got it," he said with a mock English accent. "By jove, I think you've got it." He lifted his arm. "And . . . two . . . three . . . cut."

"Good job," Peter said, coming out of the shadows over by Jenn and Luke. "Good stuff, Victor. It may be hard to cut that down to four minutes. I think you gave a lot of insight that can help many of our viewers."

"It helped me," Bailey said.

"Okay, now it's time to work on conversational skills. Kiely is over at Upstart Crow where you are going to be bussing tables."

"Why bussing tables?" Bailey asked.

"Because you'll be out working the floor with all the people. And we'll expect you to interact with them."

Bailey's stomach started to tighten until she remembered what Victor said. *It's not about me.* If she focused on the people in the chairs, instead of on herself, she could do this.

"Luke, I have some things I need to take care of here. Can you direct this shoot? You won't have to worry about the cameramen, they know how to do it, just oversee everything."

"Sure, I'd love to." Luke grabbed a clipboard and went with Peter into the office to go over details.

As he walked out, Peter turned back, propping his foot in the door to keep it from shutting. "Oh, yes, Bailey. We have a surprise for you this afternoon." As the door closed, they could hear him whistling.

"Whistling, huh?" Victor said. "My guess is that his surprise has something to do with promotional considerations paid by someone."

"Are you cynical, Victor?" Jenn asked.

"No. I just know that man."

Jenn and Bailey walked over to the commissary to get some sandwiches for the three of them to eat in the car while they drove over to the coffee shop.

"I always thought the guests on these shows had limo rides and ate in luxurious restaurants," Bailey said.

Jenn was ruffling through the bag to check that the order was all there. "Well, I know they usually put their guests up in one of the expensive hotels, but we're really fill-in guests, and I think it's pretty seat-of-the-pants this week. Do you mind?"

"Are you kidding? I'm having a wonderful time. I was just talking about reality versus perception."

"You did a great job this morning with Victor."

"I surprised myself. I enjoyed it and learned a lot too."

"Speaking of surprise, what do you think your surprise is this afternoon?" Jenn asked.

"We won't know if we don't get over there."

✳ ✳ ✳

"Here's what you do," Kiely said after they got settled at the Upstart Crow. "You just pick up empty cups and plates and remove them from the tables, putting them in those gray tubs on the stands inside that doorway." Kiely smiled. "Simple, huh?"

Bailey nodded. But it was far from simple to converse with strangers when a camera followed you every step of the way.

"Yes, except that you need to chat with everyone. If they engage you in conversation and there's an empty chair, sit down for a minute or two, okay?"

Bailey frowned. "But isn't that butting in?"

"You'll have to judge that with each customer. Remember what Victor taught you this morning. This is your room. You own it. You are here to take care of these people."

Bailey started clearing the tables, tentatively at first. *It's not about you.* "How are you today?" she asked one woman as she picked up her latte cup.

"I'm doing well," she said, sounding surprised. "Thanks for asking."

That was easy enough. As Bailey moved to the next table, she picked up a coffee cup and noticed the man was staring out the window. "Don't you love the first roses of the season?" she asked.

He seemed startled. "I'm from the Midwest and hadn't even noticed roses. We won't get our first roses for a few weeks." He smiled as she moved off.

As Bailey put the dishes into the tub in the back room, Kiely stopped her. The cameras moved in closer. "That was a whole conversation. It wasn't so bad, was it?"

"No." Bailey rearranged the dirty dishes to make more room. "It's easier when you have something to do—like picking up dirty dishes—and when you focus on the people." Bailey couldn't help wondering why the people in the coffee house were not fazed by the cameras. You'd think they'd figure something was up. But this was Los Angeles, after all. Cameras were everywhere. Bailey figured they'd probably notice when Luke came up and gave them a release form to sign after they'd been filmed.

As the afternoon went on, Bailey had less and less trouble talking to customers. She felt herself developing a take-charge attitude as she moved here, there, and all over the room. Knowing that Jenn and Luke were there helped. Most of the time they shared a table in the corner when Luke wasn't talking to the film crew.

"Make one more contact and we'll be going," Kiely said.

The only person with an empty cup was the young woman in the corner. She wore a cute outfit—a short, lightweight pink tweed jacket over a beige tank top and jeans. At first, her looks put Bailey off. She looked so sophisticated. It made Bailey self-conscious.

It's not about you, Bailey. "Hi," she said. "Can I take your cup?"

"Sure."

An empty chair sat at her table. Since this was the last encounter in front of the camera for today, Bailey slid into the chair. "Are you local?"

"I'm actually from cyberspace." The girl smiled a normal smile.

Bailey didn't know what to say next. Had she picked the only weird patron in the whole shop to sit with? How did one go about extricating herself from an uncomfortable situation like this?

"So, Bailey, have you found a date for the prom, yet?"

Bailey looked around to make sure Jenn and Luke hadn't left. Luke smiled. How did this woman know her name? Even worse, how did she know about Bailey's dateless situation?

"It is Bailey, right? Or should I call you, Dateless and Defeated? Maybe, Trapped in Tinseltown? How about, No Runs, No Hits, Just Errors?"

"You've got to be kidding!" Bailey managed to close her gaping mouth. "I know who you are. You're Ask Angela from *Metro Girl Magazine*."

The woman laughed as the camera rolled. "I am. You should have seen your face, Bailey. Speaking of cyberspace, I apologize for not answering your e-mails. It's no excuse, but I get hundreds and can only pick a couple for the column."

"That's okay. When I didn't hear from you I found someone I could ask who could make things happen." Bailey didn't tell Angela that it was once she started praying that she'd stopped writing Ask Angela. "How did you know about my dating do-over?"

"You mentioned *Metro Girl* in your first meeting with *Dating Do-Over*. The director called me and arranged for me to come and surprise you."

Bailey smiled. Victor was right. For promotional consideration . . .

"It's so nice to meet you in real time and to know I don't have to answer your letter now. You received a far better answer with your *Dating Do-Over* than I could ever give."

Luke stood up. "And . . . two . . . three . . . cut. I think that went well." He smiled at Bailey.

As they piled into Luke's car for the drive home, Bailey was glad the day was over. Bussing tables was hard work. Of course tomorrow she would have to endure the hard work of shopping on Rodeo Drive. Not to mention she would finally have her prom date. She knew she'd have fun with Trevor at the prom. They could go together and deepen their friendship.

How weird is this?" Jenn asked. "We're walking to school on a Thursday morning. It's almost like being a normal person."

Bailey laughed. They'd been out of school all week, but they were scheduled to do the date setup in the cafeteria this morning before heading out for their day of shopping. "Can this day possibly be any better? I could hardly sleep last night for thinking about it."

"I know. I feel a little guilty though. We're having so much fun and poor Jace has to take over the decorating committee this afternoon. I gave him a work list."

"But everything is still on schedule, right?" Bailey could hardly believe that she would not only be decorating the morning of prom, but this year she would actually be a Cinderella who got to change from decorating rags to a ball gown.

"Are you nervous about asking Trevor to the prom?" Jenn asked.

"Not like I would have been before. Ever since watching his interviews, I know he considers me a friend, and I know from his questionnaire he loves the idea of prom." Bailey smoothed out her sweater. She dressed with extra care this morning. It still didn't feel comfortable asking a guy to the prom, but she made herself think of it as part of the *Dating Do-Over* game.

"Look around," Jenn said as they entered the school grounds. "It looks like the whole school dressed for camera time."

It was true. Shirts had been pressed, hair combed, makeup applied. *Amazing.*

"What time is it?" Bailey forgot her watch. This segment was supposed to take place before school started at eight thirty.

"It's ten to eight."

"The camera crew should be here already. It looks like the entire student body is here as well. Some of them have never been at school this early in their lives."

The girls made their way to the cafeteria. Peter had decided it would be fitting for the date proposal to take place at the exact spot as the ill-fated salsa and backpack incidents.

"It doesn't look like Trevor is here yet." Jenn pointed

toward the group who normally hung around him. Sienna wasn't there either. "Do you think he has any idea you are going to ask him?"

"I don't know. He must have figured I was trying to impress him when I pretended to be a baseball fan, but then he also thought I was flirting with Luke during the game, so who knows?"

"Speaking of Luke, I've never seen him so excited as he's been about doing this assistant director job. He sat up last night mapping out plans for today. Then he got here way early this morning to meet with the crew."

"It's been so much fun spending all this time with you guys this week. Luke's been so sweet." Bailey knew she would miss spending so much time with them when this magical week ended.

"There's Kiely." Jenn pointed to an area behind the table where Bailey had sat with Trevor.

They walked over there, waving at the cameramen, Luke, and Kiely.

"Are you ready to get this one filmed so we can go shopping?" Kiely asked.

"I'm ready, but so far, no Trevor." The noise level in the cafeteria rose with each new student who pressed in. The cameramen panned the crowds to get the environmental shots they'd use in the show.

"There he is." Luke pointed toward the door. Trevor seemed surprised, as if he hadn't remembered about film crews coming to San Vincente. His may have been the only head of hair in the whole room that hadn't been moussed to perfection.

"I guess that answers the question about whether he expected to be picked," Jenn whispered to Bailey. "Isn't that cute that he has no idea?"

Bailey wasn't sure. She worried about that deer-in-the-headlights look he wore too often these days.

Luke waved to Trevor and signaled him to come over. "Roll film," he said.

Kiely had a handheld microphone. "We're here at San Vincente High School, home of our *Dating Do-Over* date of the week, Bailey Tollefson. The date we're planning is nothing less than the San Vincente prom. Bailey, you've been coached and prodded. You've learned to talk to people, and you've learned to feel comfortable in your own skin. Now comes your biggest test. Are you ready?" Kiely aimed the microphone at Bailey.

"I think so." Bailey's hands shook.

Luke had managed to jostle Trevor right up front where he stood smiling at Bailey. It helped to see him so encouraging.

"So, Bailey, who would you like to ask to be your date for the prom?" Kiely started to aim the microphone toward Bailey, but stopped and pulled it back. "Oh, yes . . . one little detail. *Dating Do-Over* pays for everything: the prom, the dinner, the dress, the tux, the limo, even the photos."

Applause broke out all across the cafeteria.

"So, Bailey, who's the lucky guy?" This time Kiely did point the microphone toward Bailey.

Bailey smiled at Trevor. "I'm hoping Trevor will be willing to go with me."

Everyone clapped again.

Kiely turned the microphone toward a stunned Trevor. "So, Trevor, after taking a shower in salsa and ending up bruised and battered by our Bailey, are you willing to take the chance?"

Trevor didn't say anything for a moment. "I . . . I

can't. I mean thank you for picking me, but . . ." He turned and walked away, nudging his way through the crowd.

Stunned faces all around the room must have reflected the shock on Bailey's face. Had she just been shot down in front of an audience of millions? She felt the heat creeping up her neck.

Luke made a signal to the cameramen and came up next to Bailey, taking the microphone from Kiely. "Trevor may not be available to attend, but I'd be honored if you'd do me the favor of letting me accompany you to the prom."

Bailey looked up at Luke's face. Was he just doing his job as assistant director and trying to save the show? No. She didn't think so. They were friends. Real friends. At this moment she couldn't think of another person she'd rather go with. She smiled at Luke. "I'd love to go with you."

A ripple of ohs and ahs erupted across the room.

Kiely took the microphone. "All of us strike out once in a while on the way to our perfect date, but sometimes that disappointment just points us to someone better." She put an arm around Bailey. "What do you say, girlfriend, shall we go shopping?"

"And . . . two . . . three . . . cut," Luke said, motioning with his hand.

"Let's go." Kiely handed the microphone to Luke as she turned toward Bailey. "Luke, Peter, and the crew will meet us at our first store. We need to swing by the studio and pick up Claudia."

The three of them, Kiely, Jenn, and Bailey, walked out toward the front of the school. They didn't talk, but Kiely stopped a couple of times to sign autographs.

Since the bell had not yet rung for first period, half the school followed them.

"Look, Bailey," Jenn pointed at a gorgeous white stretch limo. "You finally got your limo."

Bailey smiled but didn't say anything. Once they were inside, Kiely turned to Bailey. "Are you okay?"

"I don't know. That was the most embarrassing moment of my life. To ask a guy to the prom in the first place, but then to do it in front of the whole school . . ." Bailey sighed and shook her head. "I'm not even going to think about when it airs in front of the whole nation. I used to think nothing was worse than not being asked to the prom." She closed her eyes. "I was wrong. It's worse to be turned down."

"Are you embarrassed about going with Luke," Jenn asked. "I mean is it like going with a brother?"

Bailey laughed. The sound surprised her. It felt good and seemed to break the shock she'd been feeling. "No, he does *not* feel like my brother. And, honestly, I don't know why I didn't ask Luke in the first place. He's probably my closest guy friend. It's just that I didn't think he wanted to date." Bailey could still feel the heat of the blush that had come as soon as Trevor said no. "You know what I hate?"

"I can think of a number of possibilities," Kiely said.

"I hate the way redheads blush. I felt the color creep up my neck and blotch my cheeks the moment Trevor said no. I can still feel it."

Both Kiely and Jenn laughed.

"I don't know what we'll do about that segment, Bailey," Kiely said. "We could reassemble everyone at school tomorrow and reshoot it with you asking Luke.

That would spare you any embarrassment when our show airs . . ."

"But that wouldn't be honest." Bailey rode in silence for a full minute. "Plus everyone at school would know I'd reinvented the whole incident."

"They would understand," Jenn said. "Besides, it would give them one more chance to be on camera."

All three laughed, remembering the sight in the cafeteria. They talked about how funny it was to see everyone dressed for a possible on-camera appearance.

"I didn't see Sienna," Jenn said.

"I forgot to tell you. The school called my parents and asked if they wanted to press charges against Sienna for assault. They are taking her actions seriously. My parents didn't want to press charges, but I guess the school suspended Sienna for the balance of this week."

"The outcome could have been much worse," Kiely said. "I'm glad the school reacted forcefully."

"I don't know how it all got so blown up in Sienna's mind," Jenn said.

"It should help when she sees this episode." Bailey shifted on the limo seat.

"About this episode . . ." Kiely said, bringing them back to the subject on their minds. "We'll have to talk to Peter about what to do. In our planning meetings it all seemed so simple. We focused on your relationship with Trevor. All three clips featured you and Trevor." Kiely thought for a minute. "Though I think Luke was in each one."

"Anyway," she continued, "the clips were to show the sometimes funny, always disastrous encounters. Then we come along and do the dating do-over. Then you ask Trevor, and he's supposed to be overjoyed.

Then we dress you like a princess and off you go to your prom. The story line was simple and satisfying." Kiely leaned her head back onto the seat with a deep sigh, crossing arms over her chest. "Now the story has changed completely."

"That's what I hate about real life," Jenn said. "It's never as good as the fairy tales."

"I wish I knew what was bugging Trevor." Bailey had been worrying about this since they left school. "Something is just not right. I can feel it."

"You're not mad at him?" Kiely asked.

"No." Bailey was surprised at the question. "You met him and interviewed him, Kiely. He's one of the nicest guys you'll meet. Something is up."

"We need to pray for him," Jenn said.

"I have been." Bailey was glad Jenn was praying as well.

Kiely shook her head in disbelief. "This story line gets further and further away from the clichéd prom romance with every minute." She remained quiet for a while, then said, "Maybe we should just follow the real twists and turns and see where this takes us."

Bailey smiled. "You mean sort of like life?"

✻   ✻   ✻

"How are you doing, Bay?" Luke put an arm across her shoulders as soon as she got out of the limo at the store.

"I'm fine except for worrying about Trevor, wanting to give you a big hug for saving me, and excited about shopping all at the same time."

"I like the big hug option," he said, letting that teasing grin of his spread across his face. "I was serious, though, about being honored to go with you to prom. I told you how I've shied away from dating, but I'm confident we could go to the prom together and still grow our friendship without it getting all weird."

Bailey turned and hugged him. "I take that as a compliment, Luke. I know we'll have a wonderful time with Jenn and Jace. It'll be the best." And she meant it.

Kiely and Claudia finished their impromptu meeting with Peter. He came over to Bailey. "Are you really okay with us airing that last segment?"

"I am. As Victor would say, 'It's not about me.'"

Everyone laughed.

"There are teens all across this country who've been disappointed like me. Isn't it a better story to tell the truth and let them see that the teen years are not a time to be thinking life is over because of an unrequited love or an unrequited crush or whatever?" When she looked up she saw that one of the cameramen had been filming her. *Good. It was the truth.*

"Shall we get started?" Kiely asked, pointing toward the door of the store. "Claudia's inside, and she's chosen several dresses for each of you to try."

Bailey straightened her back and stuck out her chin. "It's a tough job, but someone's got to do it."

Primed for Prom

13

When they walked into the store, Claudia was already talking to the camera. They stood out of range and watched.

"When shopping for evening wear, one of the most important elements is the foundation under your dress. This is not something we usually talk about—especially not on television—but even before you try on your dress, make sure you have selected the right undergarments to give you the proper fit."

Bailey leaned over to Jenn and whispered,

"Now I not only have to live down being rejected on national TV, but my episode will be the Proper Underwear Episode."

Jenn laughed silently.

"It's a recipe for disaster to buy a dress and think you can find the foundations later. How many days have been wasted trying to find a crisscross strap, deep armhole, long-line bra to fit a dress that's cut in places that should never be seen."

Kiely stepped in. "You do get passionate about underwear, don't you?"

"I can't believe she can say 'bra' on television," Jenn whispered.

"Have you watched TV lately?" Bailey whispered back.

Kiely continued, "Our date of the week, Bailey Tollefson, is here to find the perfect prom dress. She and her date, Luke D'Silva, will be double dating with Luke's twin sister, Jenn, and Jenn's date, Jace. We decided it would be fun to do not one, but two complete makeovers. Come on in, girls." She extended her hand to them and they walked into the area in front of the cameras. "We'll do double makeovers for double daters."

Claudia came forward and put an arm around each girl. "The nice thing about having both Jenn and Bailey is that we can play with a whole range of colors. Bailey's red hair and pale skin will look good in a totally different color palette than Jenn's dark hair and olive skin. Besides, when it comes to shopping, two are always better than one."

Peter signaled to the cameras to stop filming. "Okay, guys," he said, "while the girls try on the first dress that

Claudia selected, go outside and get a shot of the storefront, the street, and some of the shoppers. We'll cut away to that shot when we're ready to head into the shopping segment. We may use it again to promote the prom theme next spring."

As the men moved out to do the exterior shots, Claudia showed Bailey and Jenn the racks of dresses she had chosen for each of them. "I know you won't like all the dresses. That's part of our job—to look at a dress critically and talk about what works and what doesn't."

"Wow. We've got a lot of trying on to do," Jenn said. "Good thing we love shopping."

"I've already accessorized each dress for you. That's what I've been doing all week—I'm exhausted."

"Cool. We get to see what it's like to have a personal shopper. It looks like it takes all the work out of shopping and leaves all the fun." Bailey felt ready for a little fun.

"Let me explain the system," Claudia said, picking up a clipboard from Jenn's rack. "You need to go from left to right on both the dress rack and the accessories rack. The accessories, jewelry, and handbags are put together in a bag like this." She held up a heavy ziplock bag with a necklace, earrings, and a tiny beaded bag inside. "If you take the first dress on the left, the first shoes on the left, and the first accessory bag, you'll have the complete outfit."

"What about undergarments?" Jenn asked with a big grin.

"Don't even start with me." Claudia laughed. "Like I wanted to do that skivvies ditty. You know Peter . . . when the credits roll you'll see a little line that says, 'Promotional considerations have been paid for by

United Lingerie Manufacturers Association.' What does that mean? It means that Claudia has to talk serious about undergarments. Now stop torturing your fairy godmother."

"And to answer your question," Kiely said when she stopped laughing at Claudia, "there will be an assortment of appropriate undergarments in the dressing room."

"I feel like your teacher giving a lecture here," Claudia said, "but we need to work to keep the order straight on these outfits and accessories because we use this exact order to create the shopper's guide for the Web site."

"Shopper's guide?" Bailey asked.

"This is the perk manufacturers receive in exchange for their promotional considerations. If you see a dress you like on *Dating Do-Over* you can go to the Web site and find out where you can get that dress." Claudia showed them the clipboard with all the information on every item that they would try on.

"By the way," Claudia said, "the purpose of this segment is to feature prom dresses. We already know you are not actually going to choose one of these dresses. You're going to borrow a vintage dress from the Hollywood archives, but our viewers won't know that yet. By the way, since you won't get a prom dress to keep, Peter has arranged with the store to give you each a one-thousand-dollar store credit. You can come back later and choose school clothes or whatever."

"You're kidding!" Jenn and Bailey both spoke at the same time.

"Pinch me," Bailey said. "This just gets better and better."

"Okay, let's get started," Claudia said. "I'll assist

Bailey, and Kiely will assist Jenn. We'll get you anything you need. Luckily, the store has provided two sales-people to hang up after you and put the clothes back."

"I could so get used to this," Jenn said as they headed into the dressing room.

After she undressed, Bailey unzipped the side zipper on her first prom dress and wiggled it over her head. As it slid down on her body, she felt the weight of it. "Claudia, why is this dress so heavy?"

Claudia answered from outside the door. "It's fully lined and constructed couturier fashion with lots of in-terfacings to sculpt the fabric. Plus, it's a heavy silk faille."

"Oh." Bailey had no idea what Claudia was talking about. The black dress was strapless with a folded band around the bodice. She slipped on the shoes—a pair of tight black strappy heels—and black jet jewelry. Claudia had picked a beaded black clutch to go with this outfit.

Bailey came teetering out to see Kiely talking about Jenn's dress. It seemed a little low, a little tight, and was bright, bright red.

"Bailey," Kiely said, "come over here." She talked to the camera. "You can see what I was talking about with Jenn. Both of these are lovely evening ensembles and would be perfect for thirty-something women, but they are *not* prom dresses." Kiely paused.

Claudia took over. "You're right, Kiely. Too many girls make the mistake we're illustrating with Bailey's dress. Do you see it? Unrelieved black. While black can be sophisticated, too much of it sucks the energy out of a room. It's a big mistake to shroud the beauty of youth in black. And Jenn's red dress is over the top in every way—too tight, too low, too red. The dress is wearing Jenn, not the other way around."

Luke made a motion to cut and the girls headed back to change again. They did this over and over again, with Kiely and Claudia talking about each fashion and why it worked or why it didn't.

"I never knew there was so much to learn about fashion," Bailey said once they were back in the dressing room.

"Me, neither," Jenn answered from her room.

"Part of our job is to coach our viewers," Claudia said. "Victor works as our version of a life coach, Kiely is a relationship coach, and I'm the fashion coach. This kind of TV, even though it's fun, is all about learning."

"Well, I've learned so much today, I can hardly hold another new idea," Bailey said. "I can't believe I'm saying this, but I'm glad this is our last round."

As Bailey walked out of the dressing room, Claudia put an arm on her arm and drew her forward, speaking to the camera. "Can you see that this is a perfect dress for Bailey? The pale apricot is young, but sophisticated. The dress is full enough to allow her to make an entrance and command the room, but is not costume-like in any way. Remember her first black heels? They were so high we call them nose-bleeds. The heel height on these shoes will allow her to look formal and stay comfortable. That's important. If you were to poll girls about what they remember about their proms, too many would say the discomfort of too-tight dresses, over-styled hair, and blistered feet. Fashion should be fun."

Jenn stood to the side in a dress of sapphire blue. She looked gorgeous.

"Both girls look perfect, but we've decided to pass on these dresses for now. I have an idea." Kiely smiled in a conspiratorial way. "Quick, girls, change back into your clothes and follow me."

When the girls emerged from the dressing room for the last time, the cameramen had shut their cameras off and started loading their equipment. Claudia thanked the store manager and the salespeople who helped in the dressing room. She handed each one a small envelope.

"Okay, let's get back in the limo and head to the studio. Are you starving?"

Both girls nodded.

"I have a snack in the limo. Hopefully it will revitalize you with enough energy to go through the drop-dead gorgeous gowns in the archives."

"This is living," Jenn said as she leaned back against the seat. "Eating double chocolate brownies and drinking ice-cold milk in the back of a limo."

❈   ❈   ❈

Claudia already had everything prepared for them at the archives. She chose three potential gowns for each girl and fully accessorized them. "We won't film any of the detailed costume commentary on these dresses—"

"I'll bet I know why." Jenn grinned. "Because there are no promotional considerations paid for vintage dresses."

"Bingo!" Kiely laughed. "But we will film you in the gowns you choose, and Claudia will give a little background on the collection and explain why we chose vintage."

The girls played dress up for two more hours. They could hardly believe they were able to handle these pieces of history, let alone wear them for prom.

"Look at this one," Jenn said as she ran her fingers down a Fortuny-pleat gown. "Couldn't you almost believe that Garbo once wore this dress?"

Bailey enjoyed this far more than the new prom dresses.

Each girl finally settled on the perfect dress. "We're ready to model if the crew is ready," Bailey called.

Claudia came in and clapped her hands. "How did I know you'd pick those two? Come on ladies, let's do a cameo worthy of an Oscar. You need to *sweep* onto the stage," she instructed. "Bailey first."

Kiely was already on camera, so Bailey stood behind the door listening and waiting for her entrance cue. "The dresses on Rodeo Drive were gorgeous but when we learned that the theme of San Vincente's prom was Tinseltown, we knew we had to pay a visit to one of the most extensive Hollywood vintage costume archives. It's true that Bailey and Jenn will wear dresses that are merely on loan to them, but how many teens get to wear a piece of history to their prom?"

Luke made a signal and called, "Cut." He told Kiely, "We'll be using black and white stills from some of the old films showing the stars in similar costumes. It should be an exciting segment."

Claudia peeked around the door. "The girls are ready. Are you?"

Luke gave the signal for the filming to begin again.

Claudia came through the door onto a sound stage that looked like a grand Victorian ballroom. Bailey followed, trying very hard to "sweep" into the room. It was difficult to sweep when you were short, but as Claudia told her, many of the leading ladies were tiny.

Bailey's eyes connected with Luke before she saw anything else. He smiled, blinked hard, and gave her a double thumbs-up.

"Bailey looks as if she stepped off the runway of a

1930s Oscar gala," Claudia said. "She's wearing a dress of heavy silk satin, cut on the bias. The blush color of the satin can only come from being gently aged over decades. The spray of silk gardenias trails over one shoulder and is repeated at her hip. When Bailey has her salon makeover, we'll make sure she gets fresh gardenias for her hair. Pearls are the perfect accessory with this gown, so Bailey will wear a choker of pearls and pearl drops at her ears. She's wearing a pair of peau d'soie platform pumps. When Bailey descends from her limo on Luke's arm, she'll be the talk of Tinseltown."

Bailey turned slowly and moved over toward the parlor palm to make room for Jenn.

"And here's Bailey's best friend, Jenn, wearing a halter gown of ice blue tissue taffeta. The swish of taffeta over the whisper of tulle will announce her presence long before she walks into the room. She'll be wearing a silver marcasite necklace and matching earrings. Her shoes come straight from the chorus line—ankle straps with chunky heels in a blue sparkle."

Claudia put out both arms. "Don't they look wonderful?"

Luke made cutting motions. When the cameramen turned the cameras off, Luke came onto the stage. "Do you have any idea how beautiful you two look? I feel as if I stepped into an old Hollywood movie."

That was enough for Bailey. The day that had started as the worst in her life had become a day to remember forever.

And this was just Thursday. Tomorrow would be the real makeover.

The

The next morning as Claudia led the two girls into the door of one of the hottest new salons in Beverly Hills, Jenn turned to Bailey and said, "Can you believe this? It's a school day and here we are, going to get a complete makeover." She wrapped her arms around herself before she got serious again. "Let me ask you this—does it bother you that I'm hanging on to your coattails and getting everything you get?"

"Are you kidding?" Bailey said smiling. "The only reason I walked into this dream was because of your help and your brother's job. How many times in one week can I ask you to pinch me?"

Claudia introduced each girl to her hair stylist. "But before you start with hair, you're going to get a deep cleansing skin treatment."

Bailey asked Jenn to pinch her again as they lay in a darkened room, listening to music with warm towels wrapped around their faces.

"Remind me again," Jenn asked, "do we miss Calculus?"

Bailey was way too relaxed to answer. All she could manage was a "Mmmmmm."

Their hair makeover was equally wonderful—deep conditioning and a precision cut. Bailey's was styled into a side-part, loosely marcelled style. For prom, the stylist planned to use gardenias on one side to hold it back.

"Your style looks like a cross between Harlow and Marilyn Monroe," Claudia said. "Only red."

Jenn's long, straight hair was cut into layers that swept in to frame her face. Neither girl looked over-done—they just looked like themselves, only better. The makeup artist achieved the same kind of natural look. She used a light touch, emphasizing the eyes and glossing the lips. She chose warm colors for Bailey and cool colors for Jenn.

The film crew covered every step of the transformation, but by this late in the week, the girls were so used to them, they forgot they were around. Peter kept crowing about how wonderful this episode would be. By the time they said good-bye to the *Dating Do-Over* team, Bailey could hardly believe it was over. At least they would all be together the day of prom for the final filming.

"I'm still flying so high," Luke said as they got into his car, "I can hardly bear going home. Do you two want to go to Extra Innings tonight and show off your new look?"

"I'll have to call home and check, but I'm game," Bailey said.

When Luke, Jenn, and Bailey walked into the gym at church, everyone crowded around, talking about hair or makeup or asking about the show.

"I feel like a mini-celebrity," Jenn said as she and Bailey made their way to a table on the stage at the end of the gym.

"It's so funny," Bailey said, "when I did our own homegrown makeover, I felt so different, like I was posing or something. But this time it was all in fun, and I just feel like me, only prettier."

She looked around the room. One of the important things she learned was to be aware of other people. *It's not about me.*

The basketball game took up the gym floor. Luke had managed to join immediately with Jace and the regular group. Bailey loved the sound and movement of an earnest basketball game—the *boing* of the ball as it was dribbled and the scrambling from one side of the room to the other.

She looked at the kids seated there on the stage— her friends. As she looked at Jenn, she saw that her eyes focused on something in the corner of the stage and stayed there. Bailey turned to look. For a moment, her stomach tightened.

"Did you see?" Jenn asked, leaning in.

"Yes." Pastor John was seated with Trevor, praying with him.

"Are you really okay about Trevor?" Jenn asked. "In all the fun of the past two days I almost forgot."

"I'm okay with Trevor, but I'm worried about him. I still consider him a friend."

"As we sit and watch the game, let's pray for him again. We don't have to fold our hands or anything. We can watch and pray."

Before long, Trevor got up and joined the game, playing hard, running and dribbling with the guys.

When John signaled time to gather for his talk, the guys were short of breath and throwing towels around to wipe their faces.

"Ugh," said Bailey. "I don't even want to think about how gross it is to share towels."

"It's a boy thing . . . makes them closer than blood brothers," Jenn said, laughing.

Bailey got up and passed out bottles of water and soft drinks as the group settled onto chairs or on the floor to listen to John.

He went up to the board and wrote: WYSIWYG.

"Anyone know what that means?"

One of the freshmen raised a hand. "It means that the codes are hidden and anything you do in a certain computer program will display exactly as you write it."

"That's what it means, but what does the actual acronym represent?"

"What you see is what you get," answered the same guy.

"Exactly." John paused. "What you see is what you get. Last week I spoke using the acronym P.R.O.M., re-member? The O was for openness. Since then I've been reminded of this so often." He laughed. "That happens to preachers when we expound on a subject. God gives us lots of examples in our own lives where this is a problem." He pulled up a chair and sat down. "Sometimes I try to be superpreacher, to do more and more and be better and better. The whole time God is whispering to me, 'Just be yourself.'

"You may be trying to be something you are not—perhaps class clown when your world is falling apart or a teen version of Mother Teresa when you are really struggling with your faith, or like the big-man-on-campus when you suffer from insecurity." He put his hands up as if in surrender. "God wants people who are genuine. Let me give you another word: integrity. It's what we need to strive for—being a person who is whole . . . honest. The Greek word for integrity means 'without playacting or hypocrisy.' Anyone remember what Greek plays were like?"

Bailey raised her hand. She knew what John was getting at. "They used masks."

"Right. Without playacting . . . without masks." He stood up. "I made a pledge this week to peel away my masks, you know; what you see is what you get. I found a great old Yiddish proverb: 'If I try to be like him, who will be like me?' We have to try to become more like Christ, but we need to wrestle with it and be honest about where we are—not just make it look good on the surface."

Bailey heard his words with her heart. *God, it's like you're talking to me through Pastor John. I tried to reinvent myself, to pretend to be something I'm not right up to the point of deception. What you see is what you get . . . help that be me, Lord.*

"That's all I wanted to say," John said with a laugh. "Let me pray and—"

"Excuse me." Trevor stood up in the back of the room.

"Yes?" John nodded toward him.

"May I say something?"

"Sure. Come on up here."

Trevor made his way to where John stood. "You were speaking right to me, John," he said.

John put a hand on his shoulder. "I was speaking right to myself too."

Bailey thought, *And you were speaking to me.*

"I've been wearing the mask of tough guy. You know, keeping a stiff upper lip and all that. I haven't shared my problems with anyone, and it's separated me further and further from all of you."

The room had gone silent. All the movement stopped.

"When Bailey asked me to the prom and I turned her down without giving a reason, I feared then I'd never get out from behind this mask."

He let out a pent-up breath and his shoulders fell. "I want to be open with you. We have a big problem at home. My little sister, Sarah, has leukemia. Some of the time, she's been in remission and things have been hopeful, but lately . . ." He stopped, breathing in through his nose. "Anyway, we were at the end unless she went for a bone marrow transplant. I didn't want to talk about it at school because, selfishly, it was the one place I could get away from all the sad stuff. The problem is, if you don't tell anyone, pretty soon you're living a big lie and you don't have anyone to lean on."

Bailey could feel her eyes burning.

Trevor seemed to shake himself and smile. "The good news is that Sarah is scheduled for a bone marrow transplant. Money was a big issue because insurance is funny. My dad was borrowing some and things were looking more and more possible when Bailey got on *Dating Do-Over* and they offered to pay me to use our . . . mishaps." He smiled at Bailey. "I didn't tell them why, but I squeezed every single dollar I could out of them. They were really wonderful, and it was enough to give my family a running start on the cost."

"Trevor shared some of this with me last week," John said, "and our staff prayed all this week."

Prayer. And I happen to fall into Dating Do-Over, *which gives Trevor enough money* . . . Bailey couldn't even take it in.

"But then, when I walked into the cafeteria Thursday morning and Bailey asked me to the prom—on the same weekend as Sarah's hospital stay—my mask kept anyone from knowing why I couldn't go." He turned to Bailey. "And without meaning to, I hurt a friend."

"You know one of the best things about sharing our struggles?" John asked. "We get a whole army to pray for us. Prayer changes things, Trevor."

"I'm beginning to see that."

❋　　　❋　　　❋

After the meeting was over, Trevor came over to where Bailey stood with Jenn, Luke, and Jace. "Bailey, will you forgive me?"

"I already have. I knew something was wrong. Jenn and I have been praying for you without knowing what it was."

"Would you mind if I told the team at *Dating Do-Over* about this?" Luke asked. "That sounds weird, but the show is watched by millions of viewers and just like we feature products, our director likes to feature ideas. By explaining in a little segment why you turned Bailey down, you'll immediately raise awareness for cancer research and . . . what is it—the donor registry?"

"Yes." Trevor thought about it. "I'll ask my parents, but I think they'll say yes." He laughed. "Sarah was so jealous when she found out I was going to be on *Dating Do-Over*. If I could get her on camera—hair or no hair—she'll be the happiest girl in the hospital."

Luke thought for a while. "I think we can do it. I'll let you know."

"And I won't even hold them up for money this time," Trevor said with a grin.

15

Get the red carpet rolled out, and let's get out of here." Jenn had been giving orders nonstop since early morning, but here it was two o'clock and they were finished. The ballroom had been decorated. The flickering lights had been tested and were even more effective than they'd hoped.

"This will be the first time in the history of our school that the decorators were not in jeans as the prom guests arrived." Bailey ran a hand through her messy hair. Claudia would be picking them up in an hour for the trip back to Beverly Hills. Just enough time to get home and shower.

"How nice will it be to have our own personal dresser back for prom?" Bailey asked.

"No kidding. How do we go back to reality after this?"

An hour and a half later, the limo pulled up at the salon and the fun began all over again. As Bailey finally pulled her dress over her head and shimmied it into place, she felt beautiful. But beautiful in a real way—no more pretending.

"The limo has gone to pick up Luke and Jace. They'll come here to pick you up," Kiely said. "Of course, the camera crew is in place."

Prom. Bailey couldn't believe it really happened after all these years of decorating and going home to spend the evening with Mom and Dad. Now she was not only going, but she was going with her best friends.

"It's funny," she said to Jenn. "Prom used to seem like the unreachable goal. Now I see that sometimes these events loom way too large in our lives."

"You're saying that now, after we've just been pampered and dressed in an experience that's once in a lifetime?"

"I'm not saying I haven't enjoyed every minute of this, but I've learned that the people surrounding these things are more important than the milestones themselves."

"Hmm," Jenn said. "That's something to remember for graduation, isn't it? You're saying it's not the marking of time that is as important as the people stuff— like saying good-bye to our friends and thanking our parents?"

The limo pulled up, and from where they sat inside the salon Bailey could see Luke and Jace step out. She'd never seen Luke look so good. Both of them looked amazing in their vintage tuxedos. The cameras followed them, but the guys seemed oblivious.

Kiely opened the door. "Gentlemen, your dates . . ."

Jace went over to Jenn to present her with a corsage of baby roses.

"You look even more beautiful than I imagined," Luke whispered in Bailey's ear, as he gave her a wrist corsage of gardenias. To the camera he said, "She looks like she stepped out of a Ziegfeld classic—beautiful."

Bailey's stomach did a little flippy thing. Every girl needs to hear the word "beautiful" at least once in her life.

"Everyone ready?" Luke asked. "We have several stops before we can hit that red carpet."

They climbed into the limo for the ride to Jace's house. His family and grandparents gathered around and took photo after photo. Luke finally got them all back into the limo for the ride to Bailey's house. The D'Silvas were there with Bailey's family so the prom-goers posed for even more photos, and Bailey let her sisters sit in the limo and have their pictures taken with Luke.

As the limo pulled away from the curb, Bailey knew she'd remember this night forever. "So, on to Tinsel-town now?"

"Not exactly," Luke said. "I have one more stop."

Jenn looked back at the van carrying the whole *Dating Do-Over* team. "Do they know about this? Will they follow?"

"Yes, they know," Luke said.

They drove for almost twenty minutes, and it seemed to Bailey, in the opposite direction of the prom. When they finally came to a stop and got out at the hospital, Bailey guessed what was coming. She reached on tiptoes to kiss Luke on the cheek. "Do you know how wonderful you are?"

For once, Luke was speechless.

Bailey wondered what the hospital folk thought when they saw the four of them, dressed like Hollywood celebrities, trailing a whole television production team. When they finally reached the right room, Luke went in first and motioned for everyone else to come in.

Trevor's face lit up when he saw everyone. "This is too cool. I want to get pictures with you guys. And the timing is perfect. Tomorrow, nobody would have been allowed in to see Sarah." He stopped. "By the way, this is my sister Sarah, who's been bugging me about being on *Dating Do-Over* ever since she first heard about it."

"Well, guess what," Peter said. "I'm the director and those are the cameras and you are going to be on our program."

Sarah smiled and clapped her hands.

"These are my parents," Trevor said.

After the introductions, hospital personnel began crowding into the room. Bailey almost laughed to see it. *Bring a camera and they will come.*

Peter signaled to the cameras while Kiely put an arm around Trevor and spoke into the camera. "You may have wondered why Trevor turned down Bailey's offer of a date. We found out he already had a date for prom night with one of the sweetest girls in his life—his sister, Sarah."

Sarah smiled and waved at the camera.

"Sarah's been in the fight of her life, and tonight she turns the corner as she gets ready for her bone marrow transplant which begins tomorrow."

Luke stepped forward. "Sarah, I brought you the same flowers I brought for Bailey." He put them on her wrist. "We are praying for you and pulling for you."

Sarah whispered her thanks but the words were nothing compared to the look on her face.

Trevor reached out a hand to Luke and then hugged Bailey. "Sarah's battle was the one thing I couldn't talk about until my friends gave me their unconditional friendship. When I could finally be open, much of the fear eased. I guess sharing our fears makes them easier to bear."

"*Dating Do-Over* is about the perfect date. We think this quintet of teens and this hospital setting may actually be the most perfect date we've ever arranged. And of course, when we arrange a date, we pay for that date."

Trevor's dad put a hand up to his mouth.

"San Vincente Hospital is donating all the hospital costs so that Sarah's date with life will be free." Kiely held out a hand and the hospital administrator came forward with an oversized check to hand to Trevor's dad.

Luke leaned over and whispered, "Promotional considerations have been paid for by . . ."

Bailey couldn't help the smile that broke out on her face.

"And *Dating Do-Over* will pick up any other costs not covered by insurance." Kiely moved to the side and the cameras pulled back.

Everyone talked at once. Sarah kept her eyes on the

cameras, but her mom and dad could barely speak. They kept saying, "You have no idea . . ."

As everyone started clearing out, Trevor came to Luke and Bailey. "My dad is right. You have no idea what this means to us. And you have no idea what your coming means to me. This is a prom night I'll remember for the rest of my life."

As they walked out of the hospital, Bailey turned to Luke and said, "Trevor's right. This is a prom night I'll remember for the rest of my life."

Real TV series

Olivia O'Donnell wins a total fashion makeover on the hot new reality TV show *Changing Faces*. After her whirlwind trip to Hollywood, she comes home sporting a polished, uptown look. But as she deals with her overcommitted schedule and the changed attitudes of those around her, she has to face the fact that her polish is only skin deep.

Changing Faces
ISBN: 0-8024-5413-5
ISBN-13: 978-0-8024-5413-3

Best friends Chickie and Briana know everything about each other— or so Chickie thinks. But when they win a spot on the reality TV show *Flip Flop*, Briana is terrified people will find out her shocking family secret. Both girls get more than the makeover of their bedrooms, they learn a lesson in how to trust God for the makeover of their homes and not-so-perfect families.

Flip Flop
ISBN: 0-8024-5414-3
ISBN-13: 978-0-8024-5414-0